THE SAME GOD

By the same author:

THE SAME GOD

A Novel

by

JOHN JONES

HODDER AND STOUGHTON
LONDON SYDNEY AUCKLAND TORONTO

For

ANN PASTERNAK SLATER

1

Not really to the bus queue 'I say' he said, 'oh I say' as he passed by.

'I say.'

He wore gloves. He held his ladder in one hand and curbed its swinging and plunging with the other. He had been walking briskly, but now he paused. Crowded pavement. The way was blocked. He laid his head on his left shoulder and opened his mouth, and he stood entirely still. He said, 'Now isn't this fun.'

His tongue was visible. His eyes ranged warily and with devotion.

He must have noticed a gap between the boy at the end of the bus queue and the commissionaire rooted in his uniform outside Selfridge's. Because he smiled congratulation at the gap. He addressed the very space. 'Such fun,' he said. And suddenly he moved. 'It's just the greatest fun.' He was through.

Seeming outside the world as it happened to be on the seventeenth of April in the year 1947, human beings and noise, the sweet warm day and shrinking puddles, buildings, movement, blue sky—seeming elsewhere, he stepped into the road and began to cross Oxford Street slantingly towards the Marble Arch and Hyde Park.

And the boy at the end of the queue observed each step and thought how dangerous.

The boy was eighteen, perhaps he looked younger, and his name was David Trematon. A schoolmaster once proposed Delirium Tremens, hence D.T.s which was taken up by a few who were anxious to please that particular man, but the joke soon died. In any case he had left school by

7

now. Only his sister called him David all the time.

Very dangerous, he thought, and went on looking, and spooned this thought round and comfortably round while every breath came to him perfect by itself, a gift of spring to enter his life simply, to make him weightlessly happy, strong, somehow forgiven and oh, free. So he stood in the bus queue, most of him without stress or fear hoping no harm, an idle tucked-away corner in search of trouble, anyhow diversion. I'd never, he told himself, just a short ladder but over Oxford Street I'd never; and he clenched his forgotten hands over their own burden, a violin, which he sheltered against his legs in its serious case, together with a music satchel. The man had stopped. He was half-way across and now—hemmed in now by traffic—he reared the ladder up on end beside him and waited, it appeared patiently, in the middle of Oxford Street, his attention and all purposes lifted and removed.

But he is definite, David thought.

The man stood alone.

A taxi passed between them. Two or three cars. People pushing people. A post van. The man was on the move again. But more cars. Another taxi. A heavy slow municipal thing dragging brushes to sweep the road. Straining to see, David remembered something but he wasn't sure what, and then he remembered yes, it was the man's voice or rather the shudder or little death in it when he said, 'Isn't this fun.'

Oh well.

David framed a broad 'oh well' out in the sun and the surprising London breeze, because his bus was coming, drawing up now, then tea at home; 'oh well' to cover this entire scene and let go, and 'oh well' for safe across as the man reappeared and walked round the still nose of a delivery van and gained the pavement over there.

Yes but with Park Lane to negotiate if he is going where he seems to be going.

Hyde Park's a real park, David daydreamed, hide-and-seek

park, but that Lane's no lane at all. A picture came to him of the man's thick black boots, he must have noticed them. Funny with gloves, he thought, boots with gloves, but oh well—and he gave himself the dear word 'home' to hold as his bus queue began to fret and nudge forward.

Slowly.

And less slowly.

Me now. Boots and gloves. His free hand found the pole while he concerned himself to raise a foot and place it absently, just so, tenderly, inside the bus, studying his shoe and thinking country boots for country lanes.

Anyway, home.

'Then make your mind up,' said the conductor.

He strode west along the opposite pavement, treating every shop window to a hard pretending stare. But one could say—at the corner of Oxford Street and Park Lane David truly did say—this was a dangerous crossing too. It was uproar by the petrol-rationing standard of those days, and of course the traffic was two-way. Cars and specially taxis were higher off the ground then.

'A pity,' he whispered.

No wonder he failed to find him.

He walked a few steps down Park Lane to get as clear a view as possible past Marble Arch, only for a moment, a few steps, to make sure before catching the next bus home. Oh well. Then he saw him. At least he saw the ladder, a slow wagging caught his eye, the man was resting it on end again as he joined a knot of people round a red flag, and up beside the flag stood a pointing gesticulating figure, a strenuous figure on a rostrum. Talking. Or shouting rather.

Speakers' Corner. Yes, and the ladder, that will be dangerous too if...

The red flag was licking its length in the wind, a mild wind, beautiful afternoon. David crossed Park Lane and drew near enough to make out the flag's fat white letters: PADDINGTON COMMUNIST PARTY. Here was a small audience, self-conscious, too few for comfort, David felt, as he half joined it. He did not listen but he watched the speaker and found himself increasingly teased by the high stabbing finger and sagging knees, the stomach and vital seedy pomp —tugged at and teased until the likeness Beecham exploded without warning. *Beecham*. But only with 'God Save the King'. Exact and doubtless pedantic about things he really knew, David at once recorded: only with 'God Save the King', it's not fair otherwise; and from there he drifted to Mozart, Beecham's Mozart and then just Mozart, and who was composing in Vienna before Haydn and Mozart? and he remembered playing a symphony by Carl von Dittersdorf with his first orchestra, still on his quarter-size fiddle it was so long ago, and Miss Andrewes said beforehand, this is a real concert, David is the leader and he will come on after the rest of you but in front of me because I'm conducting, and Teresa how many times have I told you not to hold the rosin in your left hand? Sticky fingers, David thought, and what ages we were tuning up, and the 'may I be excused', the interruptions. Long ago. And that was me, he registered portentously, and he began to surrender all clear forms of memory, letting them meet the present air against his skin.

The speaker was shouting about Stalin. David glanced tactfully round and discovered that the man with the ladder had vanished once again. This time he was easy to find; he had moved along to the next speaker and was standing on the fringe of another small audience, the ladder held loosely and drifting round his legs.

David approached close, the closest yet except for the beginning outside Selfridge's, and gazed at, almost into the man's face. He was listening so David listened too.

This speaker was logical and quiet. He said the end was near for some. He had a Welsh accent. His subject was the influence of the stars over our lives. The man with the ladder seemed to be interested; anyhow he spent longer with the second speaker than the first.

But at last he turned on his heel and walked off, until

he reached a space quite empty of people under a plane tree. He leaned the ladder against its trunk and dusted his hands together. Then he shot his cuffs like a conjurer, so sharp and sudden that the pigeons which had been plodding after each other in figures of eight under the tree rose in a flock and left him. He looked satisfied. Next he laid the ladder on the ground, and as he pulled its legs apart David knew he had guessed right what it was for, it was a step-ladder, not the kind you prop against walls. It must have had some ledge or drawer built into it because when the man straightened up he was holding a small but official-looking box such as a station master might have charge of. Out of this he lifted a squashed soft black hat and a book with floppy covers. He poked the hat into better shape and settled it on his head, gingerly and level, the way people wear their first. The book he tucked under one arm while he set the ladder upright, gave it a testing shake and climbed to the top. He pulled his gloves on tighter. They were yellow and cotton.

He opened the book and when he had found the right place he raised his head and looked around him scrupulously. The pigeons were returning in twos and threes. Otherwise nobody took any notice.

The ladder had seemed short enough in his hand. It was too high for this purpose, David noted, back in his first thought of how dangerous, and at that moment a voice inside him announced where shame lay: in doing nothing now after watching and following. He resented it as it spoke. He did not argue or reach a decision, he approached the ladder in dread.

'Here we are,' said the man, 'at last.'

'I know.'

'We thank our stars'—with a glance towards the astrologer's meeting—'and I bet they thank us.'

David said nothing. The boots were staring bright black into his face.

'Tell me the time.'

11

'I haven't a watch.'

'I have.'

There was a pause.

'I'm attached to him,' said the man, and ran his fingers along the old-fashioned watch chain festooned low across his waistcoat. 'We look after each other. We regulate each other. I wind him up and he winds me down, and when I get too excited he fetches me a tick in the theatricals. That's not such fun.'

He was holding his person ruefully, intimately, and David said with all speed, 'I must go home.'

'Silly boy.'

The man smiled a full admiring smile and climbed backwards down the ladder. 'Silly boy.' They confronted each other.

'I must be going.'

'You haven't told me the time yet.' He indicated a pocket with the silver chain disappearing into it, and added, 'Say hullo, go on, don't be shy.'

David began to turn away.

'Silly, silly boy. I say but he's pretty, he's pretty as paint —what shall we call him?' he asked his watch, pulling it forth and consulting it.

In spite of himself David waited for an answer. The watch seemed to vouchsafe none because after a few seconds the man rapped it with his knuckles, then looked up to explain 'He doesn't like being hurried.'

'Goodbye then.'

'Keep my place,' said the man, handing over his open book and raising the watch to give it another tap, this time against the tree they were standing under. Being a plane tree it presented him with a problem. Scabs and blisters of bark were twisting outward, curling away from the trunk as if in fierce heat and almost ready to drop off. Here and there, between these crusty and unclean, moribund, unpromising surfaces, were smaller patches from which the dead skin had recently fallen, new and almost white, moist-looking and smooth. The man selected an immaculate spot and moved to tap his watch against it; but paused. He did not bring himself to touch the tree. His breath began to come in an insistent rustling pressure of sound, a papery hiss, like someone grooming a horse. He put his face even closer to the trunk and scanned every variation. 'That's life!' he abruptly declared in a public voice, and then, softly, 'My poor old friend.' He thrust his watch away. 'You see,' he continued, 'we have to do these things'—and grasping a tattered strip of bark with great stealth and circumspection, he braced himself and gave one short sharp tug.

Swinging round he noticed David and held aloft the torn morsel of tree. 'It counts as evidence,' he said.

'Your book,' David replied, once more preparing his escape.

The man took it in silence and remounted the ladder.

'Good people!' he began at once. And in fact there were some people. The star session next door had just broken up. The Welsh speaker himself was buttoning his coat and frowning over his spent words, but several of his audience were restless for some new thing, and they wandered over and stood to one side of the ladder.

The man edged round until he had them in front of him.

David had no idea what to expect, so he was not exactly surprised by the speech which the man now delivered. He felt bothered. This is dull in a way, he decided after a while.

The man introduced himself as 'your author', not by name. 'But not a popular author,' he went on to say, 'certainly I'm an unpopular author, I'm a by-product, this is a by-product'; and he showed all of them his book with the strip of plane tree bark acting as a marker inside it. The book was the reason for their meeting here today. He told them its name. It was a word which he pro-nounced Kalbasar. He said he would explain this later. But first he must satisfy them that he had taken every reasonable

13

step to get the book printed or otherwise known. It had been read and rejected—'not this copy' he assured them, holding it forward so they could take pleasure in its clean appearance—it had been seen by all the publishers listed in *The Writers' and Artists' Yearbook*. Editors of magazines had been sent excerpts for serialisation. He had approached various printers with the suggestion that production costs should be defrayed, with interest, out of the proceeds of sale. The Director-General of the B.B.C. had considered it for broadcast reading. Obviously he had considered it very seriously and had taken expert advice, because in the end, after a long correspondence, a specialist from the Talks Department had written on his behalf to say Kalbasar was not judged altogether suitable.

The man looked grave under the brim of his hat, and declared he was no Marxist but there could be no doubt one of the troubles was money. Theatres and cinemas and commercial radio could not, he explained, any more than printers and publishers, risk losing money; and in any case he foresaw difficulties in presenting the book through such media as film and live theatre. The other trouble was specialisation. Journals existed which were not meant to be profitable, but they each had a single field—law, medicine, poetry, chess—he mentioned a long list—and Kalbasar was not for them. 'So here we are'—and his eyes passed from one to one of his small audience. 'I'm loving this,' he said. The sun reflected a fine powdering of sweat on brow and upper lip. 'The question is,' he said, 'with all these riches, where to begin.'

'Ah!'

He was looking at a sailor.

'What ship?'

The sailor looked away. He stood beside a girl who had a cold and kept pinching her nose with a sodden handkerchief while he held her other hand. The man repeated his question, twice, smiling, his head on his left shoulder as if he nursed a monkey there, and at last the sailor answered that he was being demobilised tomorrow. He added something about civvy street. The girl made a contented sound. She looked up at her sailor and gave her nose a final nip and dismissed the grey wet ball into her handbag. This hung by a strap from her shoulder, which was a fashion of those days. The man on the ladder caught her eye and seemed to be wondering whether to say something to her. Then he addressed a remark to the sailor. He said, 'But you must have put in some sea time. You aren't what we used to call a barracks stanchion.'

The sailor glanced down at the campaign ribbons on his breast. 'Right,' he answered.

'Speak up!' the man admonished him. 'Because we all want to hear what you are going to say. Now you tell us, and everybody listen. Listen everybody. Where do you keep your paper money at sea?'

The sailor stared back at him.

'Where?' the man asked.

It was still a beautiful afternoon. The group at the foot of the ladder had grown to a dozen or more. The pigeons were back in force. 'We want to know,' the man said, and David wondered what the end would be, or why it should ever end. Nightfall in Hyde Park, moths, couples, us still here. Imagine.

The man started turning over the pages of his book.

'Paper money? Letters? Your most precious things? Safe from the sea in case you are sunk. What do you do?' With this last question the man looked up. Then he prompted, 'You go to the Sick Bay and you tell the duty P.O. you have shore leave.' He turned the book round. He had found what he was looking for. 'And you ask for one of these.'

Everyone could see.

The man ran his finger round a trade-journal sort of photograph which had been pasted in opposite the typewritten page. It was a drab photograph but clear enough. David knew what it was, roughly, and experienced very great consternation. The whole gathering registered shock.

15

In the silence a heavy fair woman holding a greyhound—she had been exercising it in the park—called out 'Here!' She then ran a severe scornful eye over the mute men round her and added 'That's enough,' with menace.

'We haven't begun,' the man on the ladder answered her, 'and when we do, we must think till it hurts. Are *you* ready to think?' he asked the sailor, and when he got no reply he went on, 'You can help us with False Appearance Eleven. There you are.' He held out the photograph as far as he could reach and displayed these words written underneath in black ink. 'We have to see each False Appearance before we can see through it. We know what this is. Do we know what it is called? What is its name? Oh goodness our poor brains, this is the first of our many meetings here, our point of entry into Kalbasar, we are travelling towards a philosophy of naming.

'Well, the manufacturers called their product "Blush of Dawn". Thus it received its name. But when they began exporting it to the continent, same manufacturer, same product, they called it "Extase". This is no accident like Cona the coffee machine which nobody, I am sure, intended should specify the female pudendum. "Blush of Dawn" and "Extase". And now listen. The thinking starts here. When they supplied False Appearance Eleven to the armed forces under government contract during the war, *they called it nothing*. The Board of Trade gave it a code number *but no name*. Well, what are we to say? Two names and no name. What *are* we to say?'

He paused to scrutinise a rare white cloud.

'What *are* we to say?' he asked, returning to his audience. 'All of us have heard about the Roman general, the conqueror, who campaigned in the eastern provinces and longed to enter the Temple at Jerusalem and see what was to be seen there. He was a wise man, he wanted to know about the God of the Jews, he knew he didn't know. He was devout too. He laid his sword aside, removed his shoes. He entered the Temple and pressed on into the

Holy of Holies, and stopped, still on tiptoe, his heart racing
—amazed. Nothing there. Nothing. Bare walls. No statues,
no pictures, nothing. He looked round again very slowly
to make sure. Then he understood that the Jewish God is
imageless.

'Jehovah is a name without a likeness. False Appearance
Eleven is a likeness, a photographic likeness'—tapping the
book—'which surrenders its name to the proliferation of
its purposes. "Blush of Dawn" and "Extase" both designate
a single human enterprise. Don't be deceived,' said the man
with sudden tenderness, 'they are humble yet true names.
They are reticent about it but of course they name the
one exploit, they state the task, the bending of the will, the
purpose. But—are you really thinking?—when airmen use
this Appearance to smuggle jewelry in, and Army dentists
mix their dental fillings in it, and sailors like our friend
here have the beautiful idea of hanging it round their
necks on a length of tarred twine to keep any small thing
safe from the sea—'

'No I don't.'

'Never mind.'

'But I don't.'

'It truly doesn't matter.'

'I'm telling you. I don't,' said the sailor angrily.

The man on the ladder wagged a gloved finger at him
and urged, 'Play fair now, no facts. Forget your own case.
We are talking metaphysics, you see, not empirical psy-
chology.'

'This bloke is fucking mad,' the sailor muttered as if
to defend himself.

'We are saying, what with smuggling and dentistry and
the hazards of the sea, and all the other purposes—we are
saying no wonder False Appearance Eleven lost its name. It
became a code number, a pair of brackets to enclose mere
diversity of purpose. We are all of us naming animals in
search of love,' said the man in a blissful half-whisper, looking about him stealthily, 'and when we have to choose

between "Blush of Dawn" which confirms one human enterprise and a code number which contains many, who can doubt the result? Nobody wants brackets round if he can have arms underneath. Life is not algebra. But (and this is a matter for the whole False Appearances section of Kalbasar) we cannot expect life's barren purposes to be upheld. And as for the upholding, we must be modest like the old Jews, we must seek to name the arms always there but never to picture them. Still less must we aspire to feel them, we are not Rousseau, and not Christians, we are certainly not humanists...'

Is philosophy an art? David wondered, exhilarated by his own ignorance as the words flowed over him, though he had heard of Rousseau. His heart grew full to soreness while the man talked on and on, and he made certain resolves. In future he would not sit with his eyes shut at the ballet. He would learn more about poetry and painting. And philosophy. Is philosophy an art? His evenings after supper must be better planned. How much there is to know, he thought, for example is metaphysics the same as philosophy? All this must be discovered. And at the same time, not longer hours at the violin, but tighter discipline. Technique, technique. I will be good.

What a beautiful day he thought, breathing consciously.

It all boils down to *work* he was deciding with slowly emerging completeness, when the man fell off his ladder.

He was up in a flash dusting his clothes. He appeared unhurt. His cotton gloves were stained and pock-marked by the gravel and his book lay spreadeagled, covers uppermost, like a dropped dinner. He's a bit fat, David thought, watching him retrieve it.

The man straightened his back and made to mount the ladder again. He hesitated and said, 'Oh I say.' He was looking over David's shoulder.

Then he said, 'So you've come.'

The group had grown to perhaps thirty. Two men stood together at the back, both wearing a trim summery uniform.

Behind again was a London County Council ambulance, its doors wide open and driver standing by—and what foresight to expect an accident! David commended. But (puzzling over the short sleeves and badges and sort of tropical white) those two aren't ambulance men, they ... One of them pounced on the box under the tree, the grey box that had contained the book and hat; and David read ALAMEIN WARD on its lid and simultaneously arrived at male nurses, that's right, a hospital somewhere.

The nurse without the box said, 'Yes, we were all wondering where you had got to. Ted and I came to look. We've been here quite a minute. We were very interested listening to what you were saying.'

'Of course,' answered the man. 'But was I entirely clear?'

'It was very interesting.'

'Did everyone take my point about Spinoza?'

'Don't you worry.'

'And the teleological suspension of the ethical?'

'Oh that.'

'You must think. Goodness, you must think.'

'Come on, old chap.'

'Time to pack it in,' said the nurse who held the box. He tapped the ladder. 'And where did this come from?'

'You must think.'

'Anyhow, time for tea,' said the kind nurse who spoke first.

'Time!'

The man had remembered something.

'A time to be born,' he cried, obviously quoting, 'and a time to die. A time to laugh and a time to mourn. A time to get and a time to lose. A time to keep silence and a time to speak. A time to embrace and a time to refrain from embracing.'

He wrapped his arms round himself and then flung them out in a gesture of rejection.

'Nutty!' said the sailor. 'What did I tell you.'

His girl gave a timid laugh but two other girls in the crowd shrieked and clutched one another.

The woman with the greyhound observed at large, 'There's all kinds of madness.'

'Come on, old chap,' said the nurse who spoke first.

'Time. When is the time to refrain from embracing?'

The man considered his own question. Then with absent care he began to climb the ladder. Both nurses laid hold of him.

'"Auld Lang Syne"!' he suddenly announced. 'We can't be sure about embracing but there's no time to refrain from holding hands. I name "Auld Lang Syne". We are all naming animals in search of love. Let's think about it and meet again next week, the same afternoon, under this tree, wet or fine. Same time. Same place. We won't forget, will we? We won't forget.'

David found himself answering, 'I'll never forget.'

Their eyes met.

'Hold hands for "Auld Lang Syne". Everyone hold hands.'

The sailor and girl let go of each other. Nobody else moved.

The man acknowledged David's violin.

'You play to confirm it and the rest of us will hold hands and sing. Wait a moment'—and he strained to reach the next step of the ladder.

'Now then, now then,' said the less gentle nurse. 'It's home for you.'

The other turned his wrist with exaggeration and, dropping surprise into his voice, exclaimed, 'Gone four already! We must look sharp or we'll be late for tea.'

'Time,' murmured the man, 'time for tea. We say "The Cup that Cheers" to confirm a fruitful purpose.' He paused and mouthed 'Blush of Dawn' as if testing this against the other, and then with a clearer expression on his face he said, 'Two true names but only one True Appearance. When we say "The Cup that Cheers" we christen the arms beneath, we name an absent hero, which is what Euripides was trying to mean when he wrote "To recognise a friend is a god".'

A new kind of silence followed which made it clear that he had succeeded, for the first time, in holding everyone's complete attention—except perhaps his own since his eyes were darting to and fro under the brim of his hat, about some business. He had one foot on the ground and the other on the bottom step of the ladder. He leaned against it in the warm sun, half supported half detained by the two male nurses. His head and neck were inclined towards his audience. He seemed to be thinking what to say next.

The silence was barely touched by 'Well now, old chap.' Indeed the author of Kalbasar smiled as if his ear had been stroked. Stroked lovingly. He smiled and turned those soft brown yet vivid eyes upon the one who had spoken. It was like answering 'Say that again.'

But in the same instant he wrenched his arms free and scrambled for the top of the ladder.

Somebody said, 'Christ!'

Another called out, 'Can I do you now, sir?'

The man slipped or was dragged to the ground. Both nurses began to handle him in earnest. He resisted them, but they were quickly joined by the ambulance driver, and in any case he could not hope to achieve much since his first care was for his book which he pressed to him throughout the struggle. He asked to be allowed to finish this week's session. He pleaded in a dreadful voice. David heard him tell the three of them, between gasps, he had not even explained what Kalbasar meant. His hat fell off. A policeman now appeared, who did not join in but held his arms out cloakingly and ushered the active group in the direction it was going anyhow, towards the ambulance. When the man saw its interior gaping to receive him he stopped being violent and collected himself to utter a general farewell and apology, also a reminder about next week's meeting. He was quite calm. But the nurses distrusted this and bundled him inside. He was still speaking, calmly speaking. The driver locked the doors.

The policeman continued his shooing motions until the ambulance was on its way. He then asked a well-dressed man in the crowd, a newcomer, if he wanted to make a statement, and receiving the answer no, disappeared too.

David picked up the hat and looked inside. It was fairly new but dark and odorous with sweat. He read the following address in it: 19 Windermere Terrace, Acton W? At the time he was not surprised to find no name, his mind was on the carefully executed curly question-mark, following it away beyond postal districts and what little he knew of Acton, to the man—it must have been he—who penned it, his speech, everything about him, all the happenings of this afternoon. Our strange world, he thought.

Here and everywhere.

Thus he raised his head and looked along the Park Lane skyline, gap-toothed from the bombs, and along again to the monumental houses further south and west, Hyde Park Mansions was it? where he had been told Mr. Churchill lived. London's tone was grey and weary and unceasingly thankful, the city went on breathing relief, and splashes of new paint caught David's eye like a promise of fame countervailing the spent energies and bitter life-soiled smell which still spoke (though the war seemed long ago) of chipped cups and stacked trollies and nights out of bed and full trains and fatuous songs. In one child's eye London was young with him and also old and honourably, unceasingly thankful. It could never be otherwise. Whereas later in his life David might be watching television, a bit drunk or just fretful, and his teens would steal upon him wrapped head to foot in sound sleep and sound hard work, and unadorned except with a few treats all simple joy to think of now, like scrambled shell-eggs, or like the scarcely audible but predictable Brains Trust on a wireless which crackled in tune with a late-lit fire. 'There's no need to look,' his wife often answered, twenty years on, 'and who switched the set on anyway?' when he had been denouncing the spectacle in front of them; and he would grow thickly silent and yield his lowered gaze inch by inch to fantasy, easing himself into a retrospect where boastful, self-pitying visions were also the public and shared character of those years. Purpose and honesty and other large words thundered through his head and roused him to sanctify the past and assume a morose, threatening, unspecific posture towards contemporary things. The habit grew of demanding how can people nowadays imagine or expect this or that, argumentatively to friends, scolding his children, and alone, poised in loathing on the threshold of a self-service shop but equally at the little chemist round the corner where he would count the brands of male deodorant and call to witness, in silent vengeful rhetoric, all the starving millions of a mad world. But he was intelligent and could not launch out thus with the fists of his mind raised and fail to awaken a lucid pain, a near-smile of recognition. The selfless form did not deceive. There might be plenty wrong outside but it was he, just turned forty, who had seen enough Christmases come round. And likewise with his frequent *I wish I had realised how happy I was then.* He knew these if-only tracks of thought for what they always and everywhere reveal—a knowledge which did not halt the indulgent course of daydream, but closed, so to say, its circuit, with the result that each variable, detailed but uncomplicated, endlessly refurbished mental pattern described the one circle of truth. He never pictured and yet he clearly saw himself as essentially defeated. He blamed people and circumstances, naturally but with no heart, for what had happened to his music; he embellished the theme he could not deepen. 'I had the talent but not the temperament,' one heard him depose domestically (talent meant musicianship, temperament the rest), 'oh!' he would elaborate, pausing to frown back through the years at his unvindicated but real gift, 'oh, think of living in hotel bedrooms—and it has got much worse with air travel—and the hackneyed programmes or otherwise empty concert halls however big a name you are, and being at the beck and call of agents. And the audiences! Those cretinous audiences! God, the audiences!' But already while he hammered this in he could feel his consciousness bend round to chase its tail, at the denying touch of reason. 'Of course I never intended to be *that* sort of soloist,' he would concede to some slightly startled guest; and then, leaning forward, with a drinker's angry zeal, 'Now tell me honestly, have you ever met a virtuoso who wasn't brute stupid?' And before the answer could strike his ears, all good sense there might prove to be in it, friendship and sense, all was poisoned, had joined the inward circle of his dance of failure; instead of listening he was executing a detail of a scroll somewhere. His health. Money. Press notices. His instrument or rather instruments, he'd had bad luck there. One or other of his teachers. The cellist of their student quartet who had emigrated to Canada—Canada! —when they were set fair on the professional road. 'Orchestral leaders, you say?' he would begin again, having caught the last words of his guest's answer, 'I was offered attractive terms myself by the reconstituted L.S.O. I told them where they could put that one. English orchestras are the best sight-readers in the world. They have to be. They get least rehearsal time.' He accused everyone and everything. But never 'the war'. He never blamed the conditions in which he first studied his difficult art. The war had penetrated and engrossed his garden of promise, unspoilt, affirmative, flecked with history being still 'the war' while it became a private myth and fell ripe into David's retrospective dream.

He heard a voice but understood no words. The voice repeated, 'Are you giving it back to him, or shall I?'

As he turned he felt something press against his trouser leg. He was observing the greyhound from above, its inadequate skin, spine, trembling flanks. It sniffed the hat. Is it as hungry as it looks, he wondered. The dog sniffed again. Then it left the hat and addressed David's sex. Fending it off in a flush of thought which was less embarrassment than Rousseau again and the undiscovered openness beyond, openness which memory would interpret as the unruthless thing in himself, the thing to do with failure—and but too the breeze, new green everywhere, London, in fact this afternoon—fending the dog off he faced the woman with the fair fluffy hair, the heavy woman.

'I will,' he said.

2

WHEN he got home his sister wasn't back, so he made the tea and waited for her.

She, Anne, was secretary to a director of a publishing firm and twice a day she walked through Covent Garden to and from her office off the Strand, which was easy because they lived in Long Acre, at the top of a bomb-damaged warehouse building. She always said the flat was the right size. 'It runs itself' was an expression of hers.

He heard the clip of her heels on the stone steps far below, and then the duller, nearer sound as stone turned to wood for the last flight; and he realised he was not going to tell her the truth about the hat.

'Look what I found in Hyde Park this afternoon.'

She was surprised. They usually kissed each other first.

'On a seat.' The sentence felt too short, and David continued, 'No one was sitting on the seat.'

She glanced up from unloading her string bag.

'Has it got a name in it?'

'No, but there's an address. I'll take it back tomorrow.'

'Where?'

'Acton.'

'Don't be silly, you'll spend half the day travelling there and back. Post it.'

'Perhaps he doesn't live there any more.'

'David my darling, are you all right?'

She stood holding a packet of something she had bought, while he watched the bag with the rest of the shopping in it shift and sink and finally settle into a string-entangled heap on the table.

'Yes,' he answered, 'quite.'

She took three strides in that sudden way of hers, and kissed him. 'Tea!' she said. They sat down to a cup each but at once decided they were hungry, so David lighted the gas on the ancient leggy cooker, named Black Prince on the oven door, and he made some toast. They ate, and then, the day being Saturday, proceeded to their weekly grand settlement. Anne did a sum among the crumbs and congealing spots of butter. She worked out the cost of their keep. Simultaneously David calculated his income for this week and subtracted fares and lunches. He used to do a variable amount of music-copying, orchestral parts mostly, at threepence a sheet, and very occasionally he performed for a fee like other prize students. Today he found his answer almost at once, the sum was simple, he murmured and grunted happily, rechecking, waiting for her. Their system was that Anne paid the rent out of her weekly wage and everything else they divided evenly. When David's earnings amounted to more than his share of expenses he did what they used to describe as strengthening the reserves, that is he paid the surplus into the Post Office Savings Bank where it was available to meet some peculiar expense like new clothes. His Royal Academy scholarship covered tuition fees and his quarter of the string quartet's account at Schott's for printed music—quite a big item in the days when they were building up their repertoire.

Anne laid down her pencil and announced she was ready. The business part was soon over. She recited her figures. David said hadn't there been some shoe repairs, and she replied they were her shoes, and he said they should be included in the week's accounts, and she decided no. Otherwise that Saturday they chatted in their largest, freest way about a set of violin strings which David had sent off to Toms in Somerset for. These undoubtedly fell within the area of the quartet's necessary commitments. There were clear precedents. All four of them had charged strings to the quartet at one time or other, for they were the pride of the Academy and the Bursar had ruled that when their individual scholarship money was exhausted, the cost of further 'necessary commitments' might be referred to him. (Colin Innes, the viola and in fact the least rich of them, had recently been helped to buy a new bow. The rehairing of existing bows certainly came within the Bursar's rule, as did train fares when they travelled to play without fee at a concert approved by any teaching professor of the Academy.)

Anyhow, David's strings. Why waste time, was Anne's question, queueing for postal orders and then applying for a refund? Toms should be asked to deal with the Bursar direct.

But David enjoyed buying postal orders, it was something to do with different colours for different values and the blistery perforated paper, and the knowledge he was getting them free in the end.

What he said was, 'I never queue for long.'

She answered in her oldest manner, 'We have all got so used to queues.' Born three years before David and now nearly twenty-two, she could command these pre-war vistas.

'I know,' he told her.

They fell silent, both sensitive to Time's auspicious presence at their table, until David observed that he would pay for new strings by cheque eventually, when he had a bank account.

'Just think,' she said, and paused. 'Oh David. But I expect you will be buying your strings somewhere else by then.'

'No,' he corrected her, emphatic and self-absorbed yet with love in his heart; 'the best strings in the world come from Somerset.'

She reached for his plate quite softly, as it were through his attention, like between branches.

'Gut strings anyhow. I'm not sure about wire.' And standing up he cleared the table and went through to his bedroom to light the paraffin heater. Then while Anne did jobs round the flat he washed up breakfast and tea. She was tidying her own room when he finished. 'I'm off now,' he stated, half round the door; and he carried his violin and music to where the hot gusty smell of oil said work work work, and he set a volume of Carl Flesch exercises on the stand, chafed the backs of his hands, pinched a tuning-fork in the very shell of his ear, each move withdrawn but alert in the habit of all real players, and away for two hours until Anne called supper.

He turned down the wick of his heater. While he twisted the toylike wheel and watched the braid of yellow light melt from the ceiling, he began to call himself a fool. He should have told her the truth about the hat. Not that he meant to tell her now. He *should* have told her.

I am a fool he repeated more firmly the next morning. The hat was beside him. He sat in a virtually empty bus on his way to the Vauxhall Bridge Road.

The bus bounded through the Sunday streets and in a minute it seemed he was standing on that wide straight pavement with Hans Neumann's cello proceeding ahead unmistakably, strapped to its owner's back. Hans stopped at the corner of Sargent Street to buy an *Observer*. David caught him while he scanned the headlines and assured himself as to some fact buried in the back pages.

'Beautiful!' Hans said, as usual without greeting, and poked the newspaper in the direction of a wheeling seagull. 'It is your River Thames.'

They walked together. Hans talked and David worried about the hat. He crushed its brim against the handle of his music satchel and resolved, if he drew a blank at Acton this afternoon, to abandon it on the bus coming home. Perhaps there had been a scandal at 19 Windermere Terrace and they would pretend the man with the ladder had never lived there. More likely they would honestly not know. Or all be out. They might simply give his present address.

Exactly, his present address!—so David lectured himself as the two of them turned off Vauxhall Bridge Road down Allitson Mews, and Hans Neumann described the Baltic beaches in summer. Exactly! If only he had told Anne the complete truth last night he could have asked her advice about visiting people in lunatic asylums. David remembered her face at supper while he was insisting on this journey to Acton. He knew she knew he was concealing something, but she was so old and wise it seemed pointless to try and be more convincing. I often feel like that about her, he told himself, and his eye wandered over the humpy brick back of the Tate Gallery, almost parallel now on the right, and he called himself fool yet again. What a waste of time, Anne had said. It was true. He ought to be copying music this afternoon. And I'll miss lunch, he added, falling behind Hans Neumann since there was not room for two abreast in the alley which ran beside the grocer's shop, off the mews, to the brown door at the back. 'And,' David concluded, raising his thought to a whisper and accusing the hat with a quick glance while Hans rattled the letter-box, 'I'm sure to play badly.'

He was wrong on the last point though it took him a few minutes to find out.

Hans opened the door and called out in German, 'We are late and we both apologise, second violin and cello.'

Standing at the top of the stairs, Gottlieb Wackernagel answered in English, 'Not late, no my friends, absolutely no.' He beckoned them up. He stood with one hand over the banister rail, his fingers round it, podgy and cosseted but tapering and much longer than they appeared to be, and beringed. 'Ascend!' he said.

They did, and David laid the hat on the floor behind the head of the bed and said simply 'Hullo, Wack' (pronounced Vack) which was what everybody called him. This room of his had a screen across the far end, the thinner end, to seal off his washing and cooking affairs. It was silent, and sultry in a sunless way, and pervaded mostly by pleasant smells from the shop store-room underneath. The ceiling was low and discoloured behind the screen. Hans Neumann always named the room—with emphasis—Wack's *Kammer*, to invoke the great chamber-music ghost of Vienna. Its wood-work, mantelpiece, window-frames, sills and so on, had a bright buttony look because of Wack's habit of pressing in drawing-pins all over the place when the fit seized him, and just leaving them there.

He proceeded to sort and distribute parts. The four stands were already in position. Colin Innes was seated and tuned up, waiting to give an A on his viola.

When David saw his own instrument his breath came like panic but quite different, he knew it was expecting him and he would not play badly. It lay hushed on its crimson velvet bed, impressed and shrouded finely in a length of silk, Anne's present from the chest of family things when he brought it home very first. It was by a Dutch maker called Van Meesen who became known as the Stradivarius of the North in his own day. By no means an illustrious violin, it possessed a small and rather pale, reedy, grieving, even cheesy tone which happened to suit David, he could only call it expressive, at least (for 'the Stradivarius of the North' annoyed him) it was without the vulgar bloom of some highly esteemed Cremona fiddles, fiddles with that Renoir tone he used to say much later in his clever drinking days, before his breakdown. It was his violin. Or rather it was on semi-permanent loan from Bartlet, the Wigmore Street dealer, through the good offices of a teacher at the Academy. He had brought it straight home from Wigmore Street and they admired it together and Anne produced the length of silk, and he played some unaccompanied Bach until she interrupted with 'O let me see again' and they turned it over between them, their heads close, and she said 'Look!' simply at the grains of resin dust that had settled on the sallow varnish during those few seconds of Bach. 'That's its belly,' he announced, holding his new joy level with their eyes, 'and you can see the sound post inside through the F hole if we get the angle right, and the label —there.' And she murmured 'What unromantic names' as they shifted and peered together. and she consoled her-

31

self with *Jacobus Van Meesen Leydenensis Faciebat* grandly inscribed there with the date 1792.

It suited him. Its weary reedy voice only turned peevish when he played badly, which was his fault. Two or three hundred pounds was its market value in 1947. When the quartet established itself, in a couple of years perhaps, he would buy it or change; but on this particular morning he would have laughed and said there was no question, as soon as he had the money he would buy it. Today there was no question.

The other three were waiting for him. David drew his chair up and entered their forethought, their tightening silent concentration, like frost but warm, their closing in towards colloquy and homage, they were about to play Beethoven.

Wack retrieved the clock from under his pillow where he always thrust it to stifle its tick. 'We are not amateurs,' he stated, turning round, and this was very high praise. 'The master directed us *sempre piano e dolce* and we did not arg him.'

The others were accustomed to 'arg him'; it was another of Wack's English misconceptions. He had learnt the language by ear, he scarcely read anything, and early on in England having heard someone say 'I won't argue' he understood 'I won't arg you' and nothing that happened afterwards could put him right. He was not stupid. His attention was elsewhere. His family were Austrian Jews, and he and they had been made to clean public buildings and scrub the streets. When he told the story he used to examine his hands with a shrug of grateful wonder at their escape from harm. Myra Hess knew his father who was a minor conductor, not much more than an operatic *répétiteur*, and between them they got Wack to Brussels on the pretext of an international competition, and from there to England. War came almost at once and he found himself on the Isle of Man, detained under Section 18B like many refugees.

There were some good musicians on the Isle of Man. Outstanding among them was Hans Neumann the cellist. Wack and he weren't and never became close friends, but they played the Brahms double concerto at an informal camp concert—'roughly ready' was Wack's term for under-rehearsed occasions—and a relationship of respect was founded on the slender though not fragile basis of that Brahms evening in 1941.

Hans had been in England longer than Wack. He was an only child. His parents jointly ran a hairdressing business in Dortmund, and at the first Nazi rumblings (there was a Jewish grandmother and one of their commercial rivals proclaimed her) they shipped him off to an English boarding preparatory school. He hated the school and made a pact with himself against England. Unlike Wack he had not been a prodigy, he had played the piano merely well for a small boy and the cello was his second instrument. But then the music master at his public school where he went in 1938 suggested he should change the cello for the oboe because the orchestra, like all school orchestras, was short of woodwind; and Hans had refused, had fought him, had shown him, had shown the school, had shown everyone, had shown 'your' England.

Section 18B was an enactment full of loopholes and unpublicised evasions. A famous violinist, who is still alive, went bail for Wack by undertaking to keep him in full-time attendance at the Royal Academy in exchange for his release from the Isle of Man. Wack brought up the case of Hans Neumann. 'This is not a usual artist,' he said. Already he had chamber music in mind, not necessarily a string quartet, perhaps a piano trio. While he nursed his plans and kept possibilities open he heard many, many young pianists. In those days he had doubts about Hans as a quartet cellist—and Hans had doubts about being led by anyone. However they both came to London in 1944, both aged nineteen, leaving behind on the Isle of Man Hans's parents who had escaped from Germany at the last

33

minute, each young man acknowledging the other and guarding his own fate. Wack's family were all dead.

Their attendance at the Academy soon became perfunctory. They were not really students, a different world was already calling them. But Wack took seriously the duty, the honour, of leading the Academy orchestra, and he was scrupulous about attending rehearsals.

One winter evening he noticed a change in the front desk opposite, a new face, and face to face—the orchestra was disposed in the old-fashioned way with first and second violins opposing. Now it so happened that the string section was rehearsing for a Bach concert, and when they divided in the nine-part writing of Brandenberg Three it became possible to appraise the newcomer. Wack said nothing then but afterwards he told Hans Neumann, 'At once I made a roughly ready judgment;' and in fact that same evening of the Bach rehearsal, instead of going home when he was no longer needed, he stayed—a most unlikely behaviour—to hear the student violas and cellos play Brandenberg Six. It had struck him there must be a link between Bach's scoring this particular concerto grosso without violins and his own finding a viola for the long-contemplated quartet—this evening of all evenings, when the elusive second violin had just declared himself. It must be written in the stars, and here he sat, Gottlieb Wackernagel, free to listen and choose, made free by Bach and destiny and (if there was a God) by Him too. He sat in the hall in his fur coat but soon told himself, surprised, what he would otherwise have expected, that there was no interest here for him. It was many months later when Lionel Tertis mentioned to him that among the few pupils of his old age was an Aberdeen boy called Colin Innes—'with red ears,' said Tertis, 'and you won't understand a word he utters.' Fork in hand, Wack was doodling with canteen shepherd's pie, whipping up crests and hummocks, driving deep paths through it. 'Of course he'll never make a soloist,' Tertis stated with a questioning lift, for even he was bothered by the fixed glossy black top of Wack's head; and he turned to his own scoured plate and articulated 'Aberdeen' in a plausible Scottish accent. 'Then apparently,' replied Wack, 'I must judge,' and next, looking up at last, 'I will request Mr. Innes to perform.' *Tertis knows*, Wack was thinking, *he is a musician still, though old, and not a talker.* That same afternoon he sought out Colin in his lodgings and by nightfall he had approached David Trematon with the first words he ever addressed to him. 'Hans Neumann will be in doubt to join us' was his warning, when David said yes to his proposal.

But Hans agreed without hesitation and at once the four began working together. They met in the Academy itself except for these Sunday morning sessions, the purpose of which was to practise sight-reading for two hours or more, and then whoever felt like it would join Wack in a big desultory meal in his chamber. Now, in the spring of 1947, their Sunday routine had recently been modified, a conspiracy was under way, they had begun the serious study of Beethoven 127. This was not a guilty secret in that no official adviser would have tried to stop them, or would have disapproved exactly, whatever his view of their readiness for late Beethoven. The fact was they did not need telling, they knew the dangers. But they also wanted to attack the virtual impossibilities of that work—the later movements were still untouched and the first one's contrapuntal weave, *sempre piano e dolce* indeed, the very clasp of Beethoven's hand was as yet only but utterly their distant hope—they trusted their secret to make them step outside their growth and change, once a week, into an absolute self-criticism.

They never discussed the fact that nobody knew what they were doing, and they never dreamed of performing 127 in public—in that respect their secret was pointless as well as innocent. Moreover Beethoven was not allowed to destroy the original purpose of these meetings. After a short rest and consultation of the clock under the pillow they went on to play at sight, meaning always to choose a small composer. Today it was Boccherini whom, being young, they underestimated, though of course the two quartets which they now traversed, omitting repeats, were done respectfully, with all attention. As Wack said, they were not amateurs.

David raised his eyes to Wack's dull ceiling and rested them there, blinking until the scaly dryness left them. Hans Neumann was chafing a cool ebony peg against the side of his head while he dusted his cello and scowled at objects. Colin was nearly packed up already.

Wack liked to serve the quartet he led. He dropped his violin in naked haste across the bed and assembled the bulky Boccherini parts, then the Beethoven underneath. He had collapsed the four stands and was pulling the chairs away from their long introversion before anyone stirred to help him. This was the very last minute of work. He stood over the fourth chair and spoke briefly about a Boccherini slow movement which had just unseated them with its awkward tissue of ornamentation—a bad, an ambiguous edition, Hans broke in, laying the blame elsewhere —and Wack disappeared behind the far screen to see about food. There was always plenty. Through one of those long forgotten technicalities he managed to have lunch at the Academy Monday to Friday and still keep his ration book intact. It was something to do with the definition of a main meal and being a legal tenant. He used his milk for breakfast and chocolate in the evenings, and otherwise he spent his entire week's ration on this Sunday meal. He gathered it together in a single raid on the shops, and now, after a short pause, summoning the others behind the screen, here it was. They stood four in a line, and considered the inert stuff.

David said he had to meet someone and could not stay, he hoped Wack didn't mind.

'Absolutely no,' said Wack, which was true since he never expected to be warned in advance about non-musical things.

Colin said it was his birthday, he was nineteen today, and he thought he would walk up to Victoria and treat himself to a good stroll round the station before returning to eat. He would enjoy that.

He and David prepared to leave.

Standing square before the table of raw food, Hans Neumann said: 'Then we shall be three, and I suggest that we ostracise the fish.' He spoke in English. This was often necessary even within the quartet, because Colin knew almost no German and David had to rely on memories of the old School Certificate, and even Wack had difficulty with Hans's northern speech.

'Let us write "fish" on our potsherds,' Hans continued, using our language to expose the deficiencies of our education. And as an afterthought, 'I am speaking facetiously, you will understand.' He bent over the food.

Also reflecting with care, Wack proposed, on the contrary, three small helpings of curried fish before the main course. He and Hans turned to some meat and bacon and a red cabbage grouped together at the other end of the table, and discussed the fish in relation to these. Colin now intervened. Fondling Wack's two eggs of the week he praised the virtues of fish baked in milk—'But can we be certain there is even any milk?' Wack interposed dramatically—a very little milk, Colin said, with cheese and eggs. On no account onion, Colin said. Curried fish, he next declared, tasted better cold.

David left the room. He was surprised when Colin caught him up. These hungry deliberations sometimes took longer than the cooking itself, even than the eating. 'It's curry,' said Colin. 'You know, I'm not going to like it.' 'At least the fish wasn't thrown away,' David replied. They walked together up the Vauxhall Bridge Road. They said goodbye outside the station. Standing in front of a row of telephone kiosks David realised that Colin must have noticed the hat, but he had said nothing. Strange, he thought, and really a bit wonderful. He entered a kiosk and dialled his own number with a warm dark sensation. Anne answered at once.

'I want to tell you the truth about that hat,' he said.

'Tell me this evening. I've brought some work home from the office.'

Nevertheless he gave a pretty complete account. She listened without interrupting, and finally urged him, 'Don't worry. And don't leave anything behind on the bus.'

3

DAVID always travelled by bus. He noticed that people on buses are nice to musicians, not for love of art, he decided, but they suspect we are hungry and possess genius.

People on the underground are different.

He jumped a west-bound bus and said to the conductor, louder than necessary, 'Do you know whereabouts in Acton I can find Windermere Terrace?' A woman asked, 'Where does the young gentleman want to go?' Windermere Terrace, Acton,' shouted the conductor. 'No,' she said, 'I don't know that one.' But the whole bus was effectively roused—in those days Londoners knew London—and David got his answer from another woman up in front.

Windermere Terrace is a row of yellow-brick houses with a single line of liver-coloured bricks over the front doors and downstair windows. All the same. Unanimous. Ah, but not quite. As David walked down the terrace, from the wrong end, from Number Eighty-something, he glimpsed bright blue, a change ahead. Number Nineteen had blue railings and a blue gate. In retrospect, every house except Nineteen was yearning for a television aerial.

He opened the gate and saw a little jungle of creepers and climbing plants making to struggle up from the area below. They stood no chance against the bricks and fell back on themselves in an incestuous moist tangle. A pit. Snakes, David thought, and looked up to see if the front door was blue too. Snakes. He returned to the gate and surveyed the straight childless street. What next? Snakes. The front door was not blue but it stood open. He approached. A strip of cardboard nipped upright between milk bottles said IN THE GARDEN. He climbed five steps and looked in and straight through and out—out of the back door in line with the front and also wide open. He paused quite a moment interpreting the rectangle of spring sunlight, a slice of tree branch across it, unnatural, but that's what it was, slow motion and beyond measuring from where he stood.

The hall and passage were dark. He aimed at the far doorway, brushing soft things, past a metal gong, holes in the carpet, then a mirror. He was getting used to the gloom, he could see his teeth. He transferred the hat from his right hand to his left. He still did not feel ready. Nothing else occurred to him to do, and he began to puzzle out a notice on the wall. It was about life-saving and artificial respiration. There were diagrams. He was seeing better all the time, he could even read the words, and he now learnt that artificial respiration is used in cases of electric shock as well as bathing accidents.

Interesting, he thought—and, somehow satisfied, he walked to the back door and from there surveyed a strip of garden, threadbare grass and an apple tree at the end in blossom with a table under it. A woman, her back to him, was busy with plates, glasses and a jug. David rapped the back door.

She turned round and remarked unaccusingly, 'You are early.'

'Not exactly. You see—'

'But you're *new*. And you're *musical*.'

David withdrew his violin and preferred the hat.

'I've just come—'

'Do tell me how you heard about us.'

'This hat. You see—'

'Ah,' she said. She took it and held it out at arm's length, and sighed.

She exclaimed, 'What *has* become of him?'

'I hoped you would be able to tell me that.'

'No. You see he was only with us a very short time, when we were beginning. You know Mr. Gedge?' David opened his mouth to explain that the hat had no name in it, but she got in first with 'Well. Mr. Gedge.' He felt looked at in a personal way. Perhaps she was reckoning his age, people often seemed to. 'Mr. Gedge,' she said once more, 'that's a long story. Have some fresh lime juice,' she suddenly invited him, and when he shook his head she added, 'with Barbados sugar.'

'I wondered about Mr. Gedge. I mean his hat.'

'The sandwiches are blended algae. We miss the sea here.' The plate was piled high but she did not offer it.

'Mr. Gedge,' David prompted.

'Yes,' she said. He noted her big veins, that wrong old blue, and remembered the bird-whitened railings and gate, and thought she's old anyhow, puckered throat and deep-groined collar-bone; and her dress classical between dancing and tennis, ankle socks, canvas shoes, made her legs and everything worse. 'Mr. Gedge read our notice in *The Advertiser*. I keep it at the front of our Minute Book. We'll be needing it this afternoon.' She went inside the house and returned with a book and a newspaper cutting. 'It's what we believe,' she said, and handed the cutting over.

THE LANGUAGE OF ACTION

So little is understood about the primary forms of human self-expression. Nevertheless. 'We feel that we are greater than we know.' All interested students are invited to attend the inaugural meeting of The Pre-Jungian Group. Thursday, 4 October, 2 p.m., at 19 Windermere Terrace, W.3. And do bring your friends.

NATURE KNOWS BEST

'I see,' David said.

'Mr. Gedge came to our first meeting. He was standing over there. "Action is self-expression and self-expression is freedom," I told them in my introductory talk—"freedom of the whole human organism and freedom of every part." I took the case of the civilised toe.' She slipped a shoe off and raised her foot. 'Look at those toes. Imprisoned. Thwarted. From infancy. In this state, how can they *express* themselves? We hear a lot about freedom and the iron curtain nowadays, but where in Europe or the United States of America will you find a toe that is allowed to realise its prehensile nature, a toe that is *free to be itself*?'

'And Mr. Gedge?'

'A new-born baby can hang by its toes, you know.'

'Mr. Gedge?'

Her wide and mild, yet keen face was turned aside now.

'Mr. Gedge stood up as soon as I had finished and told us his toes were quite happy. "And so they ought to be," he said. "They wouldn't like to be in your shoes, of course, but they aren't, they're in mine and they've got nothing to grumble about. Asking them to make themselves at home in someone else's shoes would be unkind, just as it's unkind to ask elephants to play cricket at the circus. The better they do it the louder people laugh at them." I'm sure we all realised Mr. Gedge was *sincere*. But he did make things difficult for us. He wouldn't stop talking. I called the meeting to order and said I had only taken the toe as an example. It shows the elementary failure of self-expression in modern life. "A deformed toe is a deformed toe," I reminded him, "it's unnatural," but he was already on his feet again lecturing us all. "You mustn't say unnatural, that's slapping the sea because you don't like how things are. You're afraid of accidents. Nothing in nature is unnatural but everything is accidental." He told us we must think till it hurt and went on to describe a naval Trafalgar Night dinner in the Painted Hall at Greenwich, long ago, when the menu card said *Soft Toes on Toast* for savoury. "That was an accident to the card," he said, "not to the toes—or to the roes which were delicious. It was easy to enjoy everything including the misprint. But a sensible civilised toe like yours knows how to enjoy its own accidents; it surveys its knobs and bumps and says 'There then, my world's a shoe'—not 'I'm unnatural.' Some of us," he said, "have a lot to learn from our toes. My poor landlady cannot bear to see herself naked any more, and her husband says 'Don't be silly, you are still beautiful, specially from behind;' but secretly he counts the white hairs on his own forearms."

'One or two of us laughed, I think we were wondering how he knew all this, and he turned on us quite sharply and said he hoped we were laughing at our own bodies, "because," he said, "that's no harder than courage, whereas it takes great art to make the world's pain funny." He told us about a man who gets eaten by a bear in a play, how the bear tore out his shoulder-bone and he cried for help and said his name was Antigonus, a nobleman. "Wait!" Mr. Tomsett interrupted him then. (Mr. Tomsett is just down from university. He will be here this afternoon.) "Wait a moment! Surely we ought to distinguish between things like being eaten by a bear which are accidents, and growing old and dying which are inevitable." Mr. Gedge said yes encouragingly but he—Mr. Gedge—went on to talk about everything in the world being a sort of accident and what the Greeks and Germans had said. It was hard to follow and, one must admit, rather *boring*, and I was anxious, this being our first meeting, people shouldn't be put off from coming again. So I broke in and told him, I hope tactfully—'

She hesitated. David watched the sensations chase each other across her face.

'—I said we were not a *philosophical* group, not in the *technical* sense anyhow; we had come together to promote free self-expression through the language of *action*, and *words* were only incidental. "You are very welcome," I told him, "but I'm afraid you will waste your time here." "I shan't mind that," he replied, "so long as I can be certain

43

you are wasting yours." It seems a rude thing to say now, but it wasn't then. He explained he was sometimes ill and must learn to be patient about time. He was writing a book. The reason he couldn't rest was that he must, but he hoped to find peace somewhere and would definitely be coming to our next meeting. "And let's not talk about wasting time," he said, "I have had one new idea here already," and he began again about accidents and a part of his book called False Appearances, his new idea being to include a section on the toe with a photograph of a civilised, misshapen but not unnatural toe. I'm not sure if he was teasing us.'

'I wonder what the book is called,' said David artfully.

'He told us. Its name is Kalbasar. He refused to explain what that meant until he finished the book. But a Rumanian lady who was at the meeting told me afterwards Kalbasar, spelt Kolbasa, is the Russian for sausage. I don't know why sausage. He never finished the book. He hardly spoke after that first time, but he went on coming to our meetings. Sometimes he watched us exploring our personal Nature Rhythms—individuating ourselves as we call it. He was very useful working the gramophone. And sometimes he wrote his book. He was quite happy sitting out here and later indoors when the weather got cold, and when the great frost came in January and the coal ran out he began to talk more and was full of jokes about how warm his book kept him—warmer than the language of action, he said, when we took to wearing mittens and boots in all our free expression, even dancing. He always wore cotton gloves himself, I don't know why but not for warmth.'

'And what happened to him?'

'One day he came as usual except that he brought a parcel with him. After the meeting he made a speech, his only real speech since the beginning, and said this was his last meeting, he wouldn't be able to come again after this because there was no money left. He had taken a job helping to compile a dictionary, a big one, twelve volumes,

44

and he must work in a reference library during the days and finish his own book at night. He said he had enjoyed his time with us. We all wondered what was in the parcel. He undid it just as he was going and this hat was inside. Yes this is the one. He said, "Look what I've learnt about free expression," and put it on and turned round so we could all see. We were upstairs in the drawing-room. He told us he had bought it out of his first week's dictionary money, paid in advance. He had never worn a hat in his life except a naval cap, but from now on he would often wear one and think of his friends here and this house and garden, and we were to imagine it hanging by his land-lady's front door. He showed us he had written this address in it though he didn't know the postal district. Then he put it on again and said "The language of Acton!" and the rest of us clapped him loud and long.'

And that was all she could remember.

4

ANNE listened with attention, before answering, 'It may be Smith and Nordenfeld's *Global Encyclopaedia*, I don't know any other publisher who is bringing out a dictionary on that scale. I'll write them a note this evening.'

She got a reply by return of post. Mr. Henry Gedge had contributed articles to *The Global Encyclopaedia*, and it was hoped he would do more work in the future. Smith and Nordenfeld would gladly forward any communication to him.

'They call him "the distinguished antiquarian".' David was reading the letter over her shoulder. 'So we'll be able to get his address from *Who's Who.*'

'No, he won't be there.'

'Then let's write again and say we want his address for ourselves. Why shouldn't we?'

'If he's in a mental hospital they may be unforthcoming about his address. They won't like people to think they hire lunatics. No, I'll go round to their office in my lunch hour. They are only round the corner in Henrietta Street.'

'Be careful,' said David without any idea what he meant.

He was home by four o'clock that afternoon, and in the settled Monday to Friday routine of nearly two years he washed up breakfast, in tepid water, wiped the kitchen table, rubbed the table dry with his bathtowel, and sat down opposite a stack of manuscript sheet-music and orchestral parts, to begin copying. Threepence a sheet. The hack work, the small, sane purpose, was restful. He never touched his violin between arriving home and tea.

And eventually, when his mother's travelling clock said five, he lighted the gas under the kettle—Anne would not be long now—and returned to his copying until the swell of noise roused him to prepare the round tin tray: no spoons because neither of them took sugar, but otherwise the pot, the flowery jug of milk, two cups and saucers, a sideplate to bear two fat slices of Swiss Roll cut so. The kettle spouted in full boil and David now presided over the hot damp cloud, the devotions of pouring, warming, rinsing, priming, pouring again; and tea was made. The tray, set aside, revolved nearly once on its dented bottom, then all was done and still.

They had tea in the living-room every day except Saturday when the kitchen table was used for their grand settlement. The living-room was also their hall, or if you like it was the building's top-floor landing. A heavy curtain on rings sealed off the head of the stairs and made this a good place to be. In winter it was a very pleasant experience to draw the curtain. One felt its thickness and thought about lighting the oil stove. Actually there was electricity up here and a telephone, the flat having been an office once, but they kept warm by oil. Three doors led off the living-room—to their bedrooms and the kitchen. The bath was in the kitchen. Instead of an ordinary plug it had a stopper at the end of a rod, like a plunger or simplified gear lever. Down was shut. The water made a bold roar when you lifted the stopper. There was no basin so Anne and he washed in the sink. The lavatory was on the floor below but it was their own.

She would not be long. David began a new sheet. This was always the perfect task for waiting and last moments, and today it was a straightforward bassoon part making very quick work, the easiest threepence a sheet of all, when he heard her on the stairs. Like a hundred other times he completed the bar he was at. Stop any old where and mistakes creep in. He executed a firm barline and reached for the cap of his fountain pen. His heart was quiet. The unfinished sheet would stay where it was, would be dry by after tea. He checked the tray. His bathtowel needed straightening, a dirty habit and (Anne used to go on half

47

angry) handkerchiefs aren't for rubbing the table either.

He stood in the middle of the room.

Often, hearing her come, he would throw back the kitchen door and emerge with the tea-tray as she reached the head of the stairs, and she would look surprised and pleased. He came out like that now, with the large openness of privacy, but she was not alone. The man behind her was wearing soft suède shoes or David would have heard him. The first thing is to put the tray down, David thought.

The man cleared his throat and exclaimed 'Speak—well I won't say speak of the devil—' before Anne could utter. 'We were discussing you,' he finished.

Then Anne said, 'David, this is Mr. Hammond. I saw him for a minute at Smith and Nordenfeld's this morning. He very kindly said he'd come round.'

'I'm pleased to meet you,' David said.

Hammond reshaped the convention, 'How do you do, Mr. Trematon.' To Anne he added, 'A remarkable family! I hardly dared hope there would be any good looks left for the younger brother to inherit.'

'David saw Mr. Gedge in Hyde Park last Saturday.'

'And David—may I call you David?—was deeply impressed by the encounter?'

'He dropped his hat,' said David, 'and I wanted to give it back to him.'

'Really?'

'Yes.'

'Alackaday.'

Hammond glanced covertly at Anne, then turned with comic grief to the brief-case under his arm.

'Alas for my foolish presumption.' He laid the case on the table. 'How stupid of me!' he said, filling in time while he fumbled with its clasps. 'Nowadays the only exercise I get is jumping to conclusions. Ah, here it is. I had imagined this was what you were interested in.' He drew out Mr. Gedge's book and laid it on the table.

Watching her brother, Anne suggested, 'I'm sure Mr.

48

Hammond would like some tea.'

David retired to the kitchen, cut another slice of Swiss Roll and got out a cup and saucer. At the door he remembered sugar and a teaspoon and went back for them.

Anne looked flustered as she settled her limbs to pour the tea.

What had they been saying?

David held out a plate. 'Will you have a piece of cake, Mr. Hammond?'

The other put forward a groping hand, his eyes on David, his smile level and insistent. He said, 'In fact my name is Henry. I do feel *à propos* familiarity, it ought to be everything or nothing, Christian names all round or not at all. Don't you agree with me, Anne?'

'Yes, I think so.'

'But Mr. Gedge's name is Henry.'

'Ah, David!'

A finger raised in sufficient answer to such childishness, Hammond paused. He then examined his slice of Swiss Roll like some preposterous thing. 'Do you know,' he declared, 'I believe I could manage this rather better if you found me a knife.'

'Shall we all have knives,' said Anne gently.

Hammond, David decided, was the other side of manhood, over twenty-one, perhaps even twenty-five, with that unmistakable thickening to neck and wrists and obtrusive weight to the whole presence.

'It's very strange,' he was saying—and he searched his pockets, produced matches and cigarettes, offered them round and lighted one for himself, all with scarcely a pause in his talk—'it's strange in London how you can work within a few hundred yards of someone, year in year out in the same trade, and never meet. But I think I know the reason.' He waited perfunctorily. There was no question of anyone else interrupting, contributing. But he waited. 'The reason, surely, correct me if I'm wrong, the reason is that

49

London though not exactly provincial, not like Birmingham say (if you have ever visited that terrible town), nevertheless lacks the sense of metropolitan responsibility—that's it, it's not just a social thing, it's *moral*—which you find in all the European capitals I can think of, and of course in New York. (I confess I don't know South America.) In this way London is rather like Chicago or Johannesburg, or dear old Glasgow for that matter, neither provincial nor metropolitan. Now when my House sent me to New York last winter I suppose I met everyone in publishing, top-class publishing, within a month or two. Of course New Yorkers are friendly people, bless them, but at the same time they feel it is their business—their metropolitan duty—to know who is who. That's what a capital city is for, even a bloody bleak one like Edinburgh. But what do you find in London? There you are, Anne, just across the road at Hartwell's—'

'I'm only Stephen Marston's secretary, and I haven't been there a year yet.'

'No longer than that? Ah then, with me wintering in the States, all is explained.'

I hate him, I will always hate him, David was telling himself throughout, insistently; and in what seemed a completely separate area he was puzzling what to do. He tried to spread the issue out plainly like a map and keep it still. Exactly what had happened? Anne had brought a man home. That was the nub of it. A man. But no, not *a* man, *this* man. Others had come, men and women, young and less young, to the flat, not many but anyhow of course they—both of them—had friends. Not *a* man. *This* man. Anne was not an inviter on the spur of the moment, it was not like her, David reasoned, advancing the unexpectedness of Hammond's visit as the point of difference: had such a thing happened before? He tried to recall, but very soon his search for precedents was overwhelmed by a central involuntary truthfulness. He did not hate Hammond for coming without warning. The problem must be looked at in a deeper way.

Why do I flinch from the word attractive? David squarely asked himself, reviving an ancient self-suspicion of jealousy. For a year or more, and increasingly, he had been identifying feelings which he could not call normal, adult, sensible, fair. Why should she not look nice, why be afraid of attractive? Is it logical to want her as beautiful as possible, I mean beautiful as she is, but not attractive? Is it quite sane? Think of her age, David commanded himself, she is made the same as other women at least as regards certain simple facts; and he remembered his dislike of opening the chest of drawers in her bedroom—discreet though everything always was—when she asked him to fetch something. A sinister sign, he decided. I can't be normal.

When the right man comes.

Instead of all this I ought to have a calm preconception of her falling in love and marrying happily.

When the right man comes.

He suddenly became aware of how the three of them were sitting. To be precise, he discovered his own feet tucked under his chair, and followed from there to Anne neat and sideways to the tea-tray in her best silk stockings, and Hammond, opposite himself, thighs thrust deep under their narrow table, saying 'Then you cannot even be sure if you are orphans. Believe me'—clearing his throat—'I am profoundly sorry,' thus drawing Anne into further impertinent detail and survey of probabilities, the story of expensive legal attempts of long ago to trace, to bring to court— the guessing that surrounded their eloped father's life and death.

Incensed, David broke in, 'Our mother was killed.' He withheld 'in 1941' and 'in an air raid' as an example of proper reticence before strangers. He also hoped the bare confounding news would drive Hammond away.

'I have just been telling Henry,' said Anne. 'You weren't listening. *You* describe our time with the Pampered Beasts while I get some more hot water for the pot.'

David replied, 'My violin. I ought to practise.' She was

trying to hitch him to this conversation, to involve him, and he refused, he wouldn't be hitched, and Pampered Beasts was a private name. She might have respected it and said 'our cousins' or better still 'the people we lived with'.

Hammond stood up and said he must be off. Just like that. But the simpleness all left him when Anne urged 'Do stay a little' and he sat down again to weave more words and impress himself deeper. 'Thank you. But alas I mustn't essay another cup of your delicious tea. I must depart—even if David were to find himself at leisure.' Nevertheless he went on to tell a story about Kreisler leaving his own wedding early in order to practise, to which David replied Kreisler was the laziest of the master violinists as everybody knew, and Anne said she had never heard Kreisler play.

She likes him, David thought, which is more serious than me hating him—if the two things can be kept separate.

He doubted if they could, and set about considering Hammond through Anne's and his own eyes at once. The places he had been to. Or said he had. His clothes. His height. His easy voice. A clear light fell on his having called publishing a trade. This was the thing, more important than the gallantries. A trade. The modesty that was not itself. Feeling it full of menace, David thought I can see him Anne's way too. He is sophisticated.

It must be stopped.

He thrust his legs out and down, heels first, recklessly. They did not touch Hammond, nor were they positively meant to, they struck the ground with a noise which could not be an accident. So, banging and scraping, David rose to his feet, enclosing the noise in more noise, in real action.

'Anne!'

He was affected by her anxious face and could only repeat 'Anne!', more softly.

She leaned forward on her sharp elbows.

'Anne, have you forgotten Wack is coming to supper?'

'No of course not. But it isn't six o'clock yet.'

Hammond looked at his watch and began to collect himself.

'Please don't go.'

She seized the milk-jug handle as though it afforded a visible reason why Hammond must stay.

He smiled at her and went on with his preparations. He inspected his suit for crumbs, patted his pockets, returned Mr. Gedge's book to his brief-case. He settled his shoulders with a testing shrug.

He looked so very clothed.

'I wondered—' Anne began. Then she burst out, 'I was going to ask you if you could stay to supper.'

'I should like to very much.' He looked at his watch again. 'I have one or two things I must do, and to tell you the truth, I always like to have a bath and change before dinner.'

'Supper,' she corrected him.

'Or supper.'

'That will be nice.'

'O yes!' He turned and stood soldierly straight before her. 'At what hour shall I present myself?'

'Come around eight. David practises for two hours every evening. And leave your case behind if you like.'

He gave a brisk tight bow like Schnabel's, though his body was an entirely different shape.

'It has been delightful meeting you both. And I cannot tell you how much I am looking forward to this evening.'

And away he went.

David stared after him down the stairs, puzzled and a bit disarmed by the sincere tone of his last words. When Anne said 'You mustn't behave like that' it was hard to know what to answer.

'I'm sorry.'

He hoped she would speak.

'Anne, I really am sorry.'

'Yes,' she said. 'I wonder if there will be enough to eat.'

'Well, I didn't ask him to stay to supper.'

'No you didn't'—she was angry at last—'but you were so rude I couldn't help inviting him.'

'Look how he talked. And how he stood there and bowed. He was laughing at us.'

'No he wasn't.' And after a pause she said vaguely, but with great firmness, 'I expect he learnt all that at Oxford or somewhere.'

'You didn't like him did you, Anne?'

'Not very much,' she said, and hurried into the kitchen.

5

HE collected the tea things and followed after her, and having satisfied himself that she was not angry any more he tiptoed into his bedroom carrying Hammond's brief-case, and laid it on the bed and closed the door with both hands.

The book weighed nothing as he drew it out. When he considered this fact it became heavy. He scrutinised it. Marvellous to have it, he thought, and how stupidly he had behaved towards Hammond. The same stains. The same curl to the paper cover. And yet it was quite new. And yet again the edge of the pages was greasy. All those pages, he thought. Many. Hundreds. How many hundreds? The book fell open. Page 473. He could see why 473, there were fragments of plane tree bark still trapped inside.

An extraordinary receiving silence drew him down towards the page, and he began to read.

When Anne put her head round the door he was standing doing nothing. Actually he was deciding the right thing was either to stop or go back and begin at page one as Mr. Gedge must intend. 'You are an untidy boy, David,' Anne said. She meant the book and brief-case on his bed. Then she told him it was cold in here and he ought to light his oil lamp before he practised. 'I should have started already,' he said, partly to her and the rest to himself; and beneath his concentration, while he played, one memory yeasted and rose: the resolve made at the foot of Mr. Gedge's ladder to work as never before. Discipline. Technique. One day he may hear me play, David thought, and it must be good. Discipline will leave time for metaphysics, none for Hammond. I have failed this evening, but from now on ...

He emerged, as was usual when they had someone to supper, in time to lay the table.

Anne checked everything, her lips in ghostly movement, undoing and taking off her apron by feel, counting objects, removing grains of salt and other small blemishes, very slightly redisposing. Standing behind a chair, tipping it, she murmured, 'Wack there, Henry on my right.' They both stood back to admire. It was a grateful moment, a warm ledge of the day. Except there was no need for Hammond's Christian name in his absence.

Except the whole matter was trivial, once one realised one had no time for it.

In spring and autumn, when to draw the curtain at the head of the stairs was a difficult decision. This evening they agreed to draw it after supper but before coffee; by then a wintry snugness would be appropriate. 'It's only April,' Anne said, and the fact seemed enormously happy and hopeful.

'What's for pudding?' David asked.

She did not answer his question. Instead she stated, 'We will all drink water. Wack will understand.' Which was plainly sensible since the bottle of beer they always got in when Wack was coming would not be enough for two. The water jug was already in place and full. You could smell cooking. David knew what that was. He repeated, 'What's for *pudding*?'

'Well, you remember the tin of peaches,' she said, 'the tin in the American food parcel, the one we divided at the office. I told you about it, you remember.'

David did remember, and was anticipating peaches and probably home-made ice cream, was about to speak, but they got no further because the front door opened and closed with a bang far below, and a familiar shout; and David started down the stairs calling childishly 'Oh Wack, oh good it's you,' while behind him Anne was saying she had forgotten to ask Henry to let himself in.

Wack pressed his hair down and told them there was a tempest outside. He was perfectly dry. He then disrobed slowly and sat in his usual chair, while Anne went into the kitchen and evidently threw a window up to confirm the high noisy wind. Returning, she said they must listen for the door-knocker, the workmen still hadn't come to mend the bell; and she explained about Hammond.

'I'm very sorry,' David said.

'Absolutely no,' replied Wack, and politely expressed a wish to meet their new friend. 'But I must tell you both— you, Flower of London, but you also David because you have not yet heard—the news is very hot—about the parents of Hans.'

It transpired that Hans Neumann's parents had abandoned the hairdressing venture which they had only recently started in Leeds, and were converting the premises into a place where, so it was hoped, people would bring dirty clothes and wash them in automatic machines owned by the Neumanns and hired out at so much a time. Having narrated all this as unshakable fact, Wack now asked 'Can it be so?'—nursing his ungloved hands and looking from sister to brother and back again.

Anne attempted to get the scene clear by asking about the hairdressing. What went wrong? Wack didn't know. 'Nothing, perhaps.' She wondered about German and English fashions. He answered listlessly and soon rather gave up. Undiscouraged (for his excitement had not been a pretence) she made a general remark about the conservatism of North-Country taste, and they all fell silent. In due course David asked what were these machines like? at which Wack revived very markedly and described at third hand from Hans Neumann, who knew from his parents, the tumbling and turning, the pipes, the sloosh and hum and the glass port-hole through which one kept in touch with events inside. He became rapidly gleeful, which often happened to him since life outside music was a holiday when it was not a chore, and he laughed and revolved his arms in mimicry and made a funnel of his fist to peer through, until something reminded him of Anne and what he no doubt defined as her sphere of interest. And then he sat quite still and told her she must not hope for one, these machines were foreign and the Neumanns were seeking a government licence to import them.

'Never with this government,' she said cheerfully.

'I'm proud of this government,' David said.

'At least we are all proud of the Third Programme,' said Wack, and they exchanged glances and fell silent again, for he had a contract to play a Mozart sonata late one night soon, and next, very possibly, the quartet would be broadcasting, for almost everything felt possible with that fine new programme and so many other beginnings, in those days when Wack came to the flat once a fortnight pretty regularly, more than Hans Neumann but less often than Colin—though having Colin was on the verge of being alone, apart from his being so very hungry and except that with him they played vingt-et-un for matches after supper.

When Hammond banged the door-knocker he proved not difficult to hear. David uncrossed his legs at once but Anne said 'I'll go' and went.

With him Hammond brought a parcel tidily wrapped, obviously a bottle. Anne looked flustered. What has he been saying to her? I don't trust him, David thought, not that it matters compared with Mr. Gedge, in fact I hate him—as the man acknowledged Wack in a little speech about Art and Europe (and what had Anne been telling him on the stairs?) and Wack replied 'My dear fellow,' and the two of them performed a stylish handshake.

It was time they sat down to eat.

Anne was held up by the bottle in Hammond's parcel.

She made a trip to the kitchen but still said nothing on her return. Wack was describing pre-war Vienna affably, grandly, all the more grandly for his mistakes of language.

'Let's have supper,' David said.

Hammond inclined his head away from Wack and asked, 'Do you have a refrigerator?'

'Yes,' said Anne. 'Why?'

'Let me confess'—he tore off the paper and set a bottle of amber-coloured wine on the table, and began again, 'Let me confess that no sooner had we parted company this afternoon than the thought presented itself—once presented it has persisted—the suspicion struck root that my reappearance now is something of an imposition. Certainly you were kind enough to invite me with a warmth that encourages me to believe I am welcome here, in your charming home.' He looked round him in a single sweep, then intently at Anne. 'Yet ought I not to reproach myself for trespassing on your hospitality, for failing to consult your convenience or to consider your ... or to reflect that I ...' He turned the label towards her. 'I hope you won't mind me bringing this along.'

She achieved a small cry of pleasure.

'It must be chilled,' he said sternly, as if warning her against too much or premature joy in his gift.

'It's lovely,' she replied, and that was enough to hoist him back into his high manner. He discoursed upon Sauternes, 'a better springtime choice than Port,' he said, and then on to Madeira and other fashions.

David had been on the point of objecting that there was insufficient time to cool the bottle. They must eat. But discovering in the course of Hammond's talk that one drinks Sauternes after a meal, he preferred, 'We haven't any wine glasses.'

'In the big trunk, David, beside my dressing-table ...'

Anne directed him to the glasses with a studied patience she almost never used against him; and the hurt went home. He attempted, head inside their family trunk, to foretell the future. 'O God,' he said aloud. Anne called through the door, 'What's the matter? Can't you find them?'

I'm a fool, he thought, really *nothing* has happened, let's just be ordinary; and he not only found the glasses, he rubbed them bright on his handkerchief before returning.

The others had moved into the kitchen. The fridge door was open and the wine stood inside. Anne's ice cream could also be seen. This part won't last long, I'll see to it, David asserted, promised himself, in the teeth of Hammond's supervising presence while the bottle of wine occupied private space in their fridge in their kitchen where the bath was and tooth-brushes among other things.

Better out there, eating. And you could see Wack was hungry.

'What!' Hammond pointed upward. 'Running a refrigerator off the light!'

David closed the fridge door and faced him.

'Why not?' he said.

'Is it dangerous?' Anne asked.

'No,' said Hammond, 'not if the connection is sound. I will look at it some time if you will allow me.'

Leave us alone, David thought. He said, 'The connection is perfectly all right.'

'Not dangerous'—Hammond continued to Anne—'but unnecessarily expensive. Perhaps you are not aware of the two-tariff system under which electricity is dispensed to us by our socialist rulers. The first and cheaper rate—ah! but I see you are not wired for power here. All is explained.'

' "Antiquarian" did we say? So we did! Well, there's an amusing story behind that.'

He folded Smith and Nordenfeld's letter and returned it across the table to Anne. Then he raised his glass—his first glass—of Sauternes and examined it mistrustfully. All dark jowl he seemed. And, laying it down again untasted, he said to Wack, 'I hope these reminiscences of friend Gedge are not wearisome to you.'

'Don't think!' replied Wack with emphasis. 'No, unquestionably.'

'The night is still young,' said Anne—which was not like her.

Hammond picked his glass up and whispered 'Château d'Yquem,' and this time he sipped the wine.

'Furthermore, dear fellow,' said Wack, 'I am looking towards your tie. Such brilliant tones are seldom seen.'

'I was wondering where I had come across it before,' said Anne. To David's subtle shame, she added, 'Isn't it one of the Household Cavalry ties?'

Hammond flushed.

'No. No. No, as a matter of fact I am wearing the Pheidippides Club tie.'

'Pheidippides?'

'Pheidippides is the name of the ancient Greek who ran from Marathon to Sparta to ask for help when the Persian army landed.'

'Hans Neumann would know, I am certain,' said Wack simply. Perhaps he thought Hammond was a timid man in need of encouragement.

'He ran so hard he killed himself—but in vain. The Spartans made excuses and never sent their army. On the other hand the Plataeans came, a thousand of them which was the entire adult male population. They had promised to help if ever the Athenians were in trouble. Young and old, all thousand fought at Marathon.'

Hammond's way of telling this tale made it hard to speak after him.

At last, smiling an odd procuring smile, he continued, But as I was saying. Pheidippides was a runner.' He shifted in his chair.

'Those men were brave,' Wack murmured, still dwelling on the story.

'The patron of our club was a *runner*.'

With an intelligent glance Anne fed him his opportunity. 'I suppose you have to go out of London to do your running.'

'In point of fact I have never—never in my life—indulged in athletic pursuits.' Having said so much he risked another very long pause. 'The Pheidippides is a dining club, and the last toast of the evening is to the memory of Pheidippides.'

'Can it be so?' said Wack, thinking aloud in his bewilderment. 'There is no shame because you cannot run. But your tie is so beautiful, I will buy the same.'

'My dear fellow, this is a club tie. If you would like me to put you up—'

'Dear fellow too, it will not be necessary because neither am I a runner.'

'Can't you see, Wack,' said David, 'it's meant to be a joke.'

'And a typically English joke, I should say. To the memory of Pheidippides and the eternal futility of violent exercise. And by the way, and just between Englishmen, David, let it be whispered that I am contemplating a slight alteration to our final toast. An addition in fact. You must give me your opinion. Would it be an agreeable thought to couple the name of Gedge with that of Pheidippides, the tortoise with the hare?'

David returned his gaze.

'Gedge's tortoise. The first section of his book. Anne told me she had caught you studying the great work when you should have been practising. Gedge's tortoise, David, the flesh made word, the inscribed shell.'

'What did Anne say?'

'Never mind what Anne said. She wants to hear the Gedge saga, you can read it in her face. (Pray don't look so serious, Anne.) She knows nothing about the tortoise, and neither does Mr. Wackernagel—Wack, if I may call you that.'

It felt as though Hammond was taking complete charge. In an attempt to oust him David plunged in and described what had happened in Hyde Park the Saturday before.

Anne then said, 'What do you think?'—a general invitation to which Wack responded by saying he understood one thing at least, which was that Mr. Gedge was a man of feeling.

Hammond cleared his throat.

62

Anne turned towards him. His lips were atremble.

'Kafka rides again.'

After that remark, which was quite on its own, Hammond began.

'It must be nearly a year since Gedge swam into my ken. Swam is something of a *mot just*, the rain was coming down in torrents, it was the middle of the morning, and he arrived in his braces with his jacket over his head, carrying a plywood box. Roberts let him in. Roberts is our retired marine who guards the office door and deals with people who come without appointments. He knows his job, you get all sorts in our trade, and he spotted at once that there were airholes bored in the side of the box. He smelt a rat. Literally! Anyhow, having put Gedge on a chair in the corner where he could drip on to the linoleum, our Roberts went to see Oliver Kirkham-Jones, one of my oldest friends. For his sins Oliver holds a watching brief over religious books (actually we publish very little religion, his main concern is with foreign rights and translations) and Roberts knew he was the right man to approach in all—shall I say—human problems. He warned Oliver about the box and agreed to hang around until they were sure everything was all right. Then he brought Gedge in.

'I wish Oliver were here, he tells this part exquisitely. Gedge dumped his box in the middle of Oliver's carpet and announced, "The philosopher of naming cannot be sure which shall come first in a concrete myth: the word, the flesh, or the deed." Then he put his jacket on, prowling round the box, shivering and shooting his cuffs in a masterly style. The other two peered through the airholes but it was dark inside and they didn't like to get too close, and there was this sinister smell of green stuff. In the end they had to confess to Gedge they were defeated. He marched up to the box and slipped a catch—like a conjurer, Oliver says, most accomplished, debonair, queer as a scoutmaster you could see at once, as a whole camp of scoutmasters—and whipped off the lid. Inside was a tortoise and some cabbage leaves.

So Roberts went away, or rather he tried to go because Gedge noticed the tattooing on his wrists and kept him talking about the marines—Gedge was a sailor once—they both said they missed the sea, but eventually Roberts escaped and Gedge settled down to tell Oliver his story. (Oliver is a specialist in madmen and top-notch at coping with them. You would be surprised how many he encounters in that job of his.)

'Apparently Gedge was down in the City some time before the war, he was walking to the Bank of England to ascertain the truth about our gold reserves, and he saw a large crowd in the street. They were watching a man on a window ledge at the top of an office building. The man was threatening to throw himself off. Some firemen had run out a ladder from their engine and one of them was at the top reasoning with him. The police held back the crowd while they stretched an awning underneath to break his fall.

'Something possessed Gedge—you know how it is with such people—to go into the building and find out where this would-be suicide worked. It turned out he had a desk in a big room with a lot of other slaves, I imagine it was a typing pool or something of the sort, and beside his desk was this very same box with the tortoise in it hidden underneath one of those canvas covers they use for duplicating machines. Gedge got hold of the tortoise and climbed out of a downstairs window inside the police cordon; and before they realised what was happening he set off up the ladder. He told Oliver he had always been smart aloft.

'The fireman at the top came down half-way to meet him. This individual must have been nearly as mad as Gedge because when he saw the tortoise he swung himself under the ladder and let our poor friend go on up.'

Hammond laughed, and then explained, 'Oliver makes a party turn out of the rest of the story. You see Gedge got so excited he began then and there to re-enact the adventure, both sides of it, standing on Oliver's desk with the tortoise at arm's length—"Don't you dare leave him behind"—and jumping across on to a chair—"Give him to me at once! I'm going to take him with me"—and so they began to argue about making a suicide pact with a tortoise. The man said it was his tortoise but Gedge doubted if any of us could claim to own another life. "We are *all* better dead," said the man. Gedge replied it might be so, but death was as chancy as everything else in the world—and he tapped the tortoise's hard shell to emphasise his point. "He will die all right," said the man, and they both looked at the ground below, "he will break like an egg."

'And now comes the punch line.'

Wack looked up sharply. The expression was evidently new to him. But he said nothing.

'Gedge replied, "A tortoise is also an egg."

'The man was taken aback, as you might expect, and asked him what on earth he meant. By the time Gedge had finished—it took him ten minutes to give Oliver a shortened version—the desire to commit suicide had melted. Or perhaps,' said Hammond, while his eyes moved from face to face and rested lastly on Anne's, 'perhaps, despite his great love for his tortoise, the desire had merely receded.'

Unwillingly, but nobody else, it seemed, would put the question, David asked, 'What did Mr. Gedge mean?'

Tortoise was testudo in Latin, Hammond said, and testudo also meant a seige-engine. Seige-engines were lumbering tortoiselike creatures which got pushed up against the walls of beleaguered towns. One such engine was constructed by the royalist forces in the English civil war three hundred years ago, to use against the city of Gloucester. The citizens watched him coming, clumsily approaching, creaking and groaning, humping and dumping, and nicknamed him Humpty Dumpty. He was propelled towards the wall until his raised further end rested on top—*Humpty Dumpty sat on a wall*—but in the night a party of citizens overturned him into a deep surrounding moat—*Humpty Dumpty had a great fall*. He was a complete wreck, and the Cavaliers had to leave him lying there:

All the King's horses and all the King's men
Could not put Humpty Dumpty together again.

The rhyme went on being recited after its origin had been forgotten, and over the centuries Humpty Dumpty turned into an egg.

'Can this be true?' asked Wack.

'I shouldn't wonder,' Hammond told him in a cold voice. 'The factual parts of his work are surprisingly sane, surprisingly competent. Oliver remarked to me that he wouldn't mind risking a small wager on the accuracy of Gedge's historical researches.'

His mind on eggs and tortoises, David said, 'Mr. Gedge's book is called the Russian for sausage.'

'Oh yes, Kalbasar,' Hammond said, inclusively but evasively. 'The whole crazy enterprise, the book I mean, begins with the tortoise-egg: the word, the thing, the story of the would-be suicide. The tortoise-egg is aimed against Wittgenstein's duck-rabbit which is a picture that can be looked at two ways, as a sitting duck or a rabbit with its ears back. That was why Gedge borrowed his friend's pet and brought it to the office. "Whatever you do," he said, "you cannot make him look like an egg." This was very important for some reason in refuting Wittgenstein. He told Oliver he had already shown his book to a number of publishers, and he was beginning to wonder whether he was setting about it the wrong way round.

'So Oliver took another close look at the tortoise and said you certainly could not mistake him for an egg (his tact in dealing with these people falls little short of genius), and he told Gedge to send us his book, which arrived next morning. Of course it was impossible. There was a lot of God in it but not the right sort for our or anybody else's religious list. And we couldn't have marketed it as a criticism of modern linguistic philosophy, though that's what it purported to be—in a way. And it wasn't old-fashioned metaphysics either. No, it was hopeless. But Oliver did notice that the factual parts, the seige of Gloucester and so forth, were quite extraordinarily well organised; and I remembered what he had told me when I was given the job—a thankless task, let me say—of finding contributors for our *Global Encyclopaedia*. It's a more difficult business than the uninitiated would suppose, getting someone to do the work for a popular encyclopaedia in a subject like history or philosophy. The established people, dons and the rest, either despise it or else they want too much money. And with the others there's always the danger they will land you in trouble by writing nonsense. I'm told it was easier in the thirties when, thanks to Hitler, there was a crowd of academic refugees ready to do anything and do it cheap. But those happy days are passed.

'As I say, I remembered Gedge and wrote off to the address he had left with us. Of course I kept my flanks guarded. I sent him a list of the sort of articles we might be wanting, and asked him to give us the first two or three when he had finished them so we could be sure he was setting about it in the right way before we engaged him for the whole series. Now the point is I didn't write this letter myself. One doesn't when one gets above the lower rungs of the ladder in our trade. I dictated it to my short-hand girl together with a dozen others to people I wanted to hire for the encyclopaedia. And it so happened that one of these was an old buffer called Geddes, a splendid professional who does science for the boys' papers and the digest magazines. Geddes is absolutely sound, and I sent a long list of articles we should be glad to have from him, ranging from nuclear fission to cancer research; and obviously there was no need to ask for samples. All would have been well if the girl hadn't misread her own shorthand and addressed Gedge's letter to Geddes and vice versa. I would have got her sacked if I had not felt I had been careless myself in failing to check the names when I signed the letters. But I was in a hurry, and so there it was.

'In a day or two we had a letter from Geddes saying he was unable to undertake any work for us. The letter was frostily worded, but I assumed he thought our terms were ungenerous and I forgot about it. (The terms I had intended for Gedge must have made him think a great deal more than that.) Geddes, I repeat, is a splendid man with far too much professional pride to hint that the subjects we had proposed were unfamiliar. In retrospect it was the money and the tentative approach, the request for sample articles, that offended him. Anyhow, when Geddes wrote like that I didn't think twice about it. Nor was I surprised to get no answer of any kind from Gedge. I assumed he had moved house or been locked up, and I set about finding other more or less worthy hacks to replace both of them. And that was the last I heard until Saturday morning.'

'This Saturday?'

'Yes, David. Hyde Park Saturday was the day. I came back from a conference with Arthur Styles—you know we are bringing out a uniform edition of his novels—and found my girl on the phone.

'"It's the Royal Oak Hospital for Nervous Disorders," says she.

'Says I, quick as a flash and witty too, "They were bound to catch up with me sooner or later"—and the party the other end must have heard cos he laughed *hun*restrained. Then says he, "We are concerned about a patient of ours, name of Gedge. I believe you know him."

'"Not exactly"—cagey-like. "I know *of* him. I've never met him."'

This new vein seemed to give Hammond pleasure. He was playing with it, it might lead anywhere. It was intolerable to David, who broke in, 'Perhaps your letter has driven him mad.'

'Aren't you being a bit previous?' said Hammond easily. But he went on to justify himself. 'No. On the contrary.

No, the truth is almost the exact opposite of what you suggest. Steady routine work is what Gedge needs, and steady routine work is what my letter gave him. Hennessy (he's the doctor in charge) was most emphatic on the phone that Gedge needs regular employment instead of this wild speculation on the loose—bad for him, as Hennessy says, and an infernal nuisance for everybody else. No, it was quite definitely a good thing that he took my letter at its face value and started work forthwith on the list of science articles I sent him. The only trouble was he plunged in much too furiously. I had expected Geddes to take three or four months even if he had nothing else to do, but it appears Gedge has nearly finished in ten weeks, and he has had the background material to mug up in reference libraries, and I gather from Hennessy he has been up to all sorts of pranks at the same time. For example he has spent the last few Sundays touring London churches and disputing in public with the parsons. He doesn't exactly interrupt, he waits for a lead. The news got round. Soon no city clergyman dared ask a rhetorical question from his pulpit.

'The position when Hennessy rang me up on Saturday morning was this. Gedge had come in two days before some way further round the bend than usual by the sound of it —they had been treating him hitherto in their outpatients department—and when they told him they were going to make him stay inside and rest he threw a fearful scene because of his work which he said wouldn't wait. They are used to that sort of thing. They produced some pills "for his headache" and put him to sleep without further ado. But he must have been more wrought up than they bargained for, because he woke in the small hours and found his clothes and got away without raising an alarm. He went straight home and continued from where he had left off with his *Global Encyclopaedia* articles, until eight o'clock or so when he fried some bacon on his gas ring and set off again taking his belongings with him in a suitcase, including Kalbasar of course, the great work. That was Friday. His landlady smelt cooking and when she came up to his room and saw he had been back she phoned the police. She knew he ought to be in hospital. In any case he left a crazy I.O.U. for his rent.

'The police and everyone else lost track of him for twenty-four hours completely. Nobody knows where he spent Friday night. Then on Saturday morning he gave himself away by sending a telegram to the hospital, addressed to all the members of his ward there, inviting them to Hyde Park that afternoon to hear him speak. When Hennessy telephoned me the hospital authorities were simply waiting to pick him up.'

'If you will excuse me—' said Anne.

He laid a hand on her hand, his on hers, as she began to rise.

'I will brew some coffee,' she said.

He regarded her earnestly and answered, 'Anne, I will never excuse you so long as all that Château d'Yquem remains undrunk.'

Their old travelling clock was stopped, David noticed, and the bottle of wine had grown a misty bloom in the warmth.

He searched for the particular poisonous insinuation of Hammond's words.

'I will drink exactly one more glass,' stated Wack in his abrupt yet ceremonious fashion.

Anne said no, and again no under pressure, and Hammond filled Wack's glass, and then David's which David drank at once. Last he filled his own, and seeing what had happened he poured more wine into David's.

He said, 'You may well ask why Hennessy telephoned me in the first place. The fact is he wanted my help. Because Gedge got it into his head, when my letter arrived out of the blue about the *Global Encyclopaedia*, that it must be connected with his own book somehow. After thinking about it he decided we were testing him over a wide range of unfamiliar subjects as a practical, experimental check on his system of philosophy. Hence the excitement. Hence the need to satisfy us with the articles—and hence the hurry, because he imagines the sooner he finishes them the sooner his book will be published, and his book is about the reality of names and events like the tortoise-egg and making people good and wise for ever and ever amen. It all makes sense in a crackpot way. And that's why Hennessy rang up, to see if we could find a means of dealing with this obsession. This Messianic zeal. We discussed various possibilities. In the end I suggested they sent round the book (when they retrieved it), the encyclopaedia articles, and anything else they could find, and I would write to Gedge and say he had already produced enough scientific material for us to form an opinion. "That may stop the frantic working," said Hennessy, "but it won't prevent him worrying about his book." So I agreed to add in my letter—you can always put these things vaguely enough to protect yourself—that I felt confident a decision would ultimately be reached regarding the book which would prove satisfactory to all parties.'

'In the end he will realise what is happening.'

'Previous again, David. The immediate problem is to bring him nearer normal. They are keeping him quiet now with sedatives, and Hennessy thinks it won't be long before he is fit to leave hospital, so long as he doesn't undertake work that makes emotional demands on him. And that's where we come in again. My idea is we should take him on to compile the indexes for our technical books. We pay by the book, not by the week or month. He will be easy to get rid of if anything goes wrong. If all goes well there will be plenty of indexing to keep him busy, and people don't exactly fall over themselves to enter that line of business. Naturally I must put my proposal up to the directors first, but I anticipate no difficulty, the hand to mouth way we rely on casual labour for indexing is not satisfactory. Our house has always been generous about this kind of thing. And if the indexing job proves too stimulating, it may be possible to find him part-time work in our packing department.

'And what about the precious book? (I know what you are going to say, David.) The answer is—wine, Anne? Change your mind. No? Wack? Then it falls to you and me, David, to finish the bottle—the answer is the book may turn out to be no problem at all, once he has settled into a routine job with us and is attending the hospital out-patients regularly. Hennessy has good hopes they will be able to change his whole attitude—reduce his interest in the book to something manageable, or even destroy it altogether. It's wonderful what they can do nowadays. We may yet see our philosopher devoting his spare time to the football pools.'

'They make a new man,' said Wack suddenly. He cupped his hands as if sustaining some precious object in the air. 'Normal you say, nearer normal, and the single work forgotten. Then we must ask to ourselves, where is Mr. Gedge?'

'Single work indeed!' said Hammond, laughing as he echoed. 'Surely we must first *ask to ourselves*, What does the single work amount to? Where is it by the way? Anne and Wack might be amused to see the sort of stuff it is.'

'I believe in Mr. Gedge's book,' said David.

Anne stared at her brother and said 'I will get the coffee' with absolute firmness. But she paused while Hammond answered him, 'Come now. You can only have glanced at it. You didn't even know about the tortoise.'

'A glance is enough. I have heard him. I spoke to him.'

'Lucky you!'

'And you have lied to him. You will all deceive him if you can.'

Anne seemed now to hesitate between bad alternatives. Touching her throat, her mother's necklace, quickly she said, 'The book is through there. Do fetch it, David'—and herself left the room.

Hammond breathed a soft 'Ah!' when he saw David returning. 'Let me see,' he said, reaching for the book, flicking over the pages, chuckling. 'There's the tortoise large as life. Look at the photograph. Those are axioms written on his shell. And here's a whole section on parthenogenesis— virgin birth to you. No photograph. And this is simply a discourse on joy.'

Majestically, surveying a remote colony of the spirit, Wack declared, 'He writes with feeling I suppose.'

'Fantastic stuff. This would amuse you, it's about a nature-rhythm society which wanted to prevent cruelty to toes. Fantastic. And to take a professional publisher's view of it'— glancing towards the kitchen door—'there's only one pur-pose, one natural function this book can serve. One pur-pose.' He fingered the thin paper. 'A fundamental purpose.'

'Give it back to me.'

David climbed to his feet.

In a trance of astonishment or fear, he was pale too, Hammond handed the book over; and at that moment Anne carried in the coffee.

'What is it, David?' she asked.

He gazed at her stupidly.

'Sit down, my darling,' she said. 'Have some coffee. You aren't used to wine. Where are you going?'

'No,' he said, and uttered a sort of lengthy cough. As he crossed the room Hammond was beginning a round-about apology. He tore the heavy green curtain aside.

'I am going to find him.'

Anne called something from behind which he failed to hear. She was in distress, he could tell.

6

THE wind had died to nothing and the stars were out. It had grown cold for some reason.

It could not be late, there was too much noise and movement, the usual night drift, in the direction of Charing Cross Road, and David stopped under a lamp-post to read his watch. It said nearly nine thirty. He felt suddenly faint and rested his head against the hard humming pole.

He was sick, copiously.

Remarkable how better he was at once. None of this felt like what he had heard about being drunk, his body was keen, his head clear and airy. That's better, he thought. Somebody was approaching. He moved away from his vomit. He felt resolute. It was exactly the opposite of being fuddled. Give us problems to solve was how he expressed it, though the *us* seemed like another person's habit of mind.

Anyhow Royal Oak lay beyond Paddington; it could not be far from Acton and Windermere Terrace and the woman with the civilised toes, not that he wanted help from her.

For above all he felt resolute. Other people, older people, were just people who were there to be dealt with firmly. He had a book to give back to an acquaintance. What could be more ordinary, more natural anyhow? Mr. Gedge was in an anxious state, he had fallen ill because of the book. One should not leave such matters overnight.

The hospital reeled with light from end to end. It looked festive and stuck, a holiday ship aground on the dark shoals of Paddington, and the main doors were actually open.

Inside it was like a ship too. Subdued. Green impressions.

74

Engines. The hidden busy crew.

A big ship, David thought.

'This way, young man, if you want something.'

Her head reached through a hole in the wall under the word RECEPTION.

'I have come to see Dr. Hennessy.'

'It's a most unusual time for an appointment.'

'I have no appointment. I must speak to him about a patient.'

'Male or female?'

'Male.'

She considered.

'In any case he may not be here.'

'I know he is here.'

'How do you know?'

'They made him come, at least they tricked him.'

'I am talking about Dr. Hennessy.'

'I am talking about Mr. Gedge,' said David.

He strode towards her.

'Then I want to see the nurse in charge of Alamein Ward.'

'The ward sister? She's on duty you know, and there's no visiting after eight. Except in emergency. And then only next of kin.'

'Mr. Gedge has no next of kin—no relatives I mean. And I am not visiting. I want to talk to somebody about him. It's important. He is my—we both—I know him.'

'Just a moment.'

She withdrew her head carefully and addressed a dusty switchboard. Her lipstick stood on a volume of the London Telephone Directory. There was a kettle and a handbag and an electric fire burning plum-red despite the stale heat everywhere. A kind of hibernation was going on.

'Oh hullo, sister. I've got a young man here—yes that's what I did say—he wants to talk to Him about a patient. Yes. No. Oh so He's not. Oh so He will. The young man says you will do.' The other answered something which made her laugh, and she groped in her handbag while her eyes roamed the ceiling. 'Mmmm yes. I'll tell the young man that.' And she rang off.

'Sister Osborne says she expects Dr. Hennessy to look in for a few minutes at ten o'clock. If you like you can wait in the night duty room across the way from Alamein. First floor; turn right at the end of the corridor; second door on your left.'

She called after him meaningfully, 'Dr. Hennessy is the Psychiatric Registrar.'

One thing at a time, David thought. He decided he would first discover what he could about the ward. It was easy to find but it proved oddly to be called M4, not Alamein, on the door itself. M4. She should have warned him. A firm rational displeasure with the switchboard woman now possessed him, and he determined to mention the matter on his way out.

M for Male presumably.

A round little window, still like a ship, brought him against the ward door, nose to glass. He remembered Wack's account of the automatic washing machines. Somehow wire netting was stretched across inside this glass. He scratched at the faintly green window and wondered how the wire got there.

And why is it there?

What can I see?

Beds.

What else?

Two hands descended lightly on his waist, and a voice said, behind him, 'Won't you come inside?'

'Are you Dr. Hennessy?'

'Yes.'

'I have come to talk to you about Mr. Gedge.'

'I was expecting you.'

'You must have got the wrong person. My name is David Trematon.'

'No. I have got the right person. I didn't know your

name,' he added, regarding David curiously, 'but I was expecting the Hyde Park boy. Pretty as paint. He's been talking. When he's conscious he talks. And you've brought his book.' Dr. Hennessy had blue eyes and profuse grey hair. He wore a white doctor's coat. He looked senior but, despite his hair, not old. 'Well met!' he suddenly said, and caught David's wrist.

'Restless—aren't you?'

'I don't think so.'

'Still at school?'

'I'm a musician.'

He turned the captive hand over.

'Violin,' David said.

'Isn't this sweating a nuisance when you play?'

'I don't usually sweat.'

'You don't usually drink either, do you—yet? Sensible to leave a few vices for your old age.'

'Why were you expecting me?'

Dr. Hennessy studied him thoughtfully without answering. At length he said 'Come on in' and opened the door.

They stood just inside.

'Your friend isn't with this lot.'

On the inside the door had no handle.

'We aren't really friends.'

'No?'

'I followed him and heard him speak.'

'Perhaps you would call yourself his disciple.'

David surveyed the two long rows of beds, thinking he's not here.

'No. I don't know.'

'Never mind.' Then Dr. Hennessy said 'We're in luck. The Normaliser is on duty. The best pair of legs in the hospital'—as if to dispel seriousness at one stroke.

He meant the nurse at the other end of the ward. She had seen them come in, and now approached.

'Sister Osborne, this is Mr. Trematon,' said Dr. Hennessy with complete correctness.

The pale young woman recited several scraps of information which the charge nurse, apparently a man, had left with her when he went off duty. Dr. Hennessy listened and said nothing. She was in a hurry although everything seemed quiet and slow inside that place. She wanted to start. 'Follow along if you like,' said Dr. Hennessy to David, 'and pretend to heed my words of wisdom, it helps a man's self-esteem. There is no need to be bored.' He pointed after Sister Osborne's retreating legs.

The three of them walked round the ward in single file, stopping only when Dr. Hennessy picked out a fever chart from the rack at the end of an iron bedstead. 'What's the score?' he said then, or 'Let's take a peep at tonight's headlines,' and he would give the chart a quick spin between his fingers to make it land on the bed itself, wheeling as it fell; and before it touched the blanket he was on the move again, head away, telling Sister Osborne his instructions. One old man did call out 'I'm still not sleeping, Doctor,' as they were passing him by with his chart unlooked at, and Dr. Hennessy told him to stick to the white pills, they worked wonders so long as you stuck to them, 'and you can always think your own thoughts, Grandpa,' he said, 'you with that long memory of yours.' Almost everybody was old. Many eyes followed the procession of three. The movement of eyes was exaggerated by the stillness of each tented shape.

Until Dr. Hennessy led the other two into the middle of the ward, and there they stopped, and he talked to Sister Osborne. David was about to interrupt, firmly, when they caught each other's eye over her shoulder, and Dr. Hennessy said, 'Through there. On his own. He will be deeply asleep. You go ahead and I will follow in a minute.'

Asleep he was, on his back, a tight band of sheet under his chin. They had put him in a cot—just like a child's cot with a catch each end of one side to let it up and down. There was no pillow. Over the top a rope net had been stretched. The mesh was unnecessarily fine if they

78

were thinking about escape, so fine David could scarcely thrust his arm through. He loosened the sheet a bit. Mr. Gedge lay very still breathing slow deep snarls. It seemed a struggle. His eyes were not quite shut. He had been sweating, but not now. 'Get well,' David whispered, and walked once round the mansize cot, it was a thing to do, and then he searched quickly through the cupboard at its foot for a sign of how they were looking after him.

Dressing-gown and slippers. So he gets up sometimes. And he must eat. And the lavatory.

There was a pair of earphones on top of the cupboard, plugged in. David held them to one ear, expecting music, but it was a parlour game. He heard the voices. And now Dr. Hennessy appeared and joined him at the foot of the cot.

'Well, what about this one?'

They stood in silence.

'Tell me. What did he talk about in Hyde Park?'

'False appearances and true names.'

'And what did that amount to?'

'In the end he wanted us all to hold hands. I believe it was really about love.'

'Love is a big subject—ask the Normaliser some time when you are feeling strong.'

David scanned the bare little room, then the cot and its net roof which looked like a protection against pecking birds.

'He said he would be speaking again this Saturday, and the one after, and the one after that.'

'No chance,' said Dr. Hennessy.

Roused by his light tone, David answered, 'But for you he would be there. Look what you have done to him.'

'Hold on, laddie. We haven't done anything except work to make him well.'

'Well! Who in the whole world is well?'

'That's another big subject. Doctors have a rough and ready answer.'

'Why shut him up like this?'

79

'Ah, that's an easier one.'

'And the smell?'

'It's the treatment, it's the barbiturate on his breath. We are sending him to sleep for ten days. We call it narcosis, not much is known yet, it's a new idea, but we have had some promising results already.'

'He must eat,' said David.

'We rouse them enough to push some liquids into them. They aren't really conscious, they surface into a kind of twilight and then down again.'

'Ten days. His nightmares. His dreams even.'

'Food is no problem.'

'Think of his dreams.'

'Don't think of them,' said Dr. Hennessy.

'I hope somebody does,' said David, hoping Anne was right and God was thinking of them.

'A doctor has to put his heart into his pocket, often,' Dr. Hennessy said, 'if he is going to do his job properly. Otherwise he will be too wrapped up in human suffering to give his patients their best chance of health. And here we have a drug which has proved itself again and again'—he paused—'in other connections. Phenobarbitone is handy stuff. We hope it will do the trick now.'

'What is the matter with him?'

Dr. Hennessy seemed to calculate.

'The word is hypermania.'

'He has strange ideas sometimes,' said David who also spoke with circumspection, but the drink was wearing off, 'is it delusions or illusions? Anyhow he has these ideas. So I wondered about paranoia.'

Again handling the words as with tongs, Dr. Hennessy uttered 'Paranoia.' Then he said, 'Well. Yes. Paranoia. To cut a long story short, the whole concept of paranoia is becoming unfashionable.'

'Unfashionable?'

'Scientifically disreputable.'

David moved nearer the head of the cot. 'I am not

criticising Mr. Gedge when I say paranoia. Quite the opposite. I expressed it badly. His book shows,' the boy said, taking the very object into both hands, 'that he is a wise man.'

'He is clever certainly. Witty. In the first few hours before we got him under he had us all rolling in the aisles. The Normaliser is his joke, he saw we were worried about the homosexual thing and he pretended we had chosen the most seductive nurse in the hospital to put him right. He pretended to flirt with her outrageously. At least how can I say *pretended*?' Dr. Hennessy went on, almost to himself. 'This elation of his is very untypical. Without doubt he is hypermanic, but the rest doesn't fit. The systematic work. The stamina. The intellectual power. You know. It's strange. It really is. He is high all the time, high but in touch. Then he spoils it all by going through the roof.'

He looked at David and said 'Yes, perhaps he is wise'— as if the possibility had just occurred to him.

'I believe he is wisest when he is highest.'

'Maybe. That's scarcely the point. When he gets up there he isn't able to live with other people.'

'It ought not to be too difficult. He wanted us all to hold hands and remember what he said and what he wanted to say, and meet again next week.'

'Now look laddie, you must understand he is ill. He isn't here for fun. Apart from everything else he is a danger to himself. I mean physically. He needs watching, you can't take your eye off him, he's better now, we don't believe in straitjackets and padded cells but we had an appalling time putting him under. If you had seen him fighting against sedation you wouldn't need to be told he was ill. He's better now. He has given up the unequal.'

After reflecting on what had just been said, and studying Mr. Gedge's face, David asked what would happen if this present treatment failed. Dr. Hennessy replied without enthusiasm that they might try psychoanalysis, and when David said he sounded unconfident he explained there was no reason to suppose an analyst could do better than a sympathetic layman who was prepared to listen to the patient's woes. He was continuing about evidence and statistics, when David broke in and asked him to repeat what he had just said.

Dr. Hennessy frowned and was silent. What he had actually said was 'sit and hold his hand and listen to his woes'. David was waiting to pounce on this and remind him of Hyde Park. Listening to each other and holding hands was exactly it. Exactly *what*, he was not yet sure. He waited. But Dr. Hennessy said nothing and for the first time David felt tired, a bit sick again, and purposeless. 'I must go home,' he said.

'Tell me,' said Dr. Hennessy.

'Yes.'

'You remember when you came into the ward.'

'Yes.'

'To see Gedge. Your Gedge.'

'Yes.'

'Friend wasn't quite right. I asked you. And you didn't like disciple either.'

David waited. He knew something was coming. Dr. Hennessy was searching to and fro on top of the cupboard; it was as if a small valuable thing had got mislaid.

'Yes,' said David.

There was nothing on top of the cupboard except the earphones.

'Tell me, are you in love with him?'

'No.'

'Don't be afraid of words.'

The bedclothes rose to a sharp peak at the toes.

'No,' said David, thinking how time changed things because a minute earlier he would have answered goodness knows what but it would not have been 'No'. And yet Mr. Gedge was unchanged, he had not moved at all. The same rising smell like old mushrooms. Snore and snore again. David gazed down into the hairy, dewy nostrils and accused himself of missing a chance. It would not return. He had seen a flower and gone home without it. He had said 'No'.

He now tried to put matters right, asking Dr. Hennessy, could they go somewhere and sit down? And the doctor led him to the night duty room opposite M4, Alamein that is, and there they talked. At least David talked and Dr. Hennessy listened but was encouraging and almost open once or twice, remarking 'That could be a good idea' after he had mentioned music. David had said Mr.Gedge might enjoy music, and whether or not the present treatment was successful, music might make him calm, not just concerts but rehearsal and all the quiet work involved. In fact David mentioned the quartet. He had a picture of Mr. Gedge listening to them and then going away and writing his book, and whenever he felt overwrought coming back again to listen some more, and they would be still struggling with the same passage and even the same phrase, Beethoven 127 very probably, and he would tease them for being slow. Anyhow David described what chamber music was like from the point of view of a serious performing standard. And Dr. Hennessy said very little, though one remark was particularly surprising and pleasing, which was that his wife would agree with him, David, about the value of music.

A slight hitch occurred later, when David said, 'And then there is my own practising, two hours every evening, and I always allow myself some unaccompanied Bach at the end.'

They were walking along the corridor on their way out.

Carrying straight on, Dr. Hennessy said, 'I wouldn't have him home if I were you.'

That was all. David left it alone and remarked that Mr. Gedge would be in hospital for some time yet, he supposed.

'Yes,' said Dr. Hennessy, 'but not as long as I should like, almost certainly. I wish he had stolen that ladder.'

This time David did ask why, and was told it would put the hospital in a stronger position, legally, for making him stay and agree to treatment if the ladder he was using in Hyde Park turned out to be stolen. But unfortunately he had bought it in a junk shop in Maida Vale.

'Tiresome!' Dr. Hennessy exclaimed—then 'To bed!' as they reached the main entrance.

David wanted to put heart into him, and showed him the book under his arm. One should remember, he said, how sensible a lot of it was, this must be a hopeful sign. In a sudden impulse he handed it over. Dr. Hennessy warned him, 'Don't expect too much.' He repeated what he had said earlier, that the case was untypical although Mr. Gedge was certainly to be classed as hypermanic. 'His age is wrong too, you know. All this is much more like a manic student in his twenties, this scribbling the truth about the universe.'

'His book is not scribbling. Everybody agrees, even Mr. Hammond—'

'Hammond!' said Dr. Hennessy, and 'Hammond!' again with a slicing gesture. 'Now there's a conceited little bastard for you. And a pretender. I wasted half a morning and two phone calls before I discovered he is just a glorified clerk in that office of his. The whole Gedge business had to be arranged again with his boss.'

Outside, David turned these words over in his mind, and tired though he was and still fearful for Mr. Gedge, he smelt blood, and his journey home was light.

7

'IT was called "Who Are the Pure in Heart?".'

'A challenging title,' Henry Hammond said.

The Reverend Crumm stirred his coffee.

'What you publishers describe—I'm told you do—as a *strong* title.'

Thereupon he stirred again, more briskly still, and laid aside his spoon. He looked deep into the whirlpool he had made. 'A pulpit can be a tight corner spiritually speaking,' he said, raising his sad eyes. 'But the battle is half won by catching their attention at the start. At the start! What am I saying! Before the start! I always say, advertise or perish. It applies to the church as much as to any other organisation nowadays, that's why we announce our sermons each week on our notice board facing the main road. Grand idea, that, I think. I don't mind admitting I take trouble with my sermon titles. Are you enjoying that?' he asked, pointing at Henry Hammond's ginger cake.

The cake was delicious, Henry Hammond told him.

'It was a family joke when the children were small: Crumm I must be but not crummy. It shows what you can make of an old saying—waste not want not—if you are blessed with just that little bit of imagination.'

The cake was delicious, Henry Hammond repeated, and he allowed himself a faint smile against this stupid old man, his host.

'The main road notice board is another case in point. As I told them at the Parochial Church Council meeting, we are casting our bread upon the waters. Spiritual bread. The waters of the world. Advertise or perish. When I first put it to them they were most reluctant—oh most reluctant.

We were at it hammer and tongs, I don't remember a scrap like that since the famous Wednesday evening interdenominational debate on the Apostolic Succession. My word that was a rough house. The Methodists sent along a very tough customer. And there was a Moral Re-Armament fellow who knew a thing or two. And a lady. We asked the R.C.s to come as well, but they refused; they said all their clergy were busy on parish work—wily birds, the Romans—so we roped in a young Logical Positivist lecturer from the university. No holds barred that evening! But the P.C.C. meeting wasn't a tea party either, and when I finally got my notice board by jove I felt I had earned it. My blood was up all right. Witness my words at the meeting. "This notice board—this advertisement—let us call a spade a spade—this advertisement will bring us up against the declared enemies of religion. It will also force the issue among some waverers and sincere agnostics. Sometimes it will cause division among *thinking Christians*. But never fear that division. A really united family can afford a quarrel now and then. And as for the others, let us face all comers with a clear conscience and a strong right arm." '

While he was quoting himself, the Reverend Crumm's mind began to wander (for he knew that speech perfectly) and settle upon his mid-morning vitamin pill. This young publisher had arrived early for their appointment, as he was about to fetch it from the bathroom cupboard. He used to take it with a cup of coffee at eleven. Had done so for the past fortnight. Too soon yet to say if he felt the benefit, a fair trial was needed. But he must not be soft with himself. The question was, were vitamins really a fad, or were they a food, like *Force*?

> High o'er the fence leaps Sunny Jim,
> *Force* is the food which raises him.

As a young curate it had always been *Force* for breakfast —and late supper often.

What bags of energy he had in those days.

'I suppose friend Gedge saw your notice board,' Henry Hammond was saying.

The Reverend Crumm pulled his wits together. He must have finished quoting himself. He answered, 'Not only did he see it, he wrote to me at length about it. No, I wasn't caught napping. I was on my toes from the moment I began my sermon.'

'Ah, dear Gedge. Who are the pure in heart? Indeed! Indeed, indeed! Before we go any further, let me tell you my end of the story.'

The vitamin pill would do just as much good with lunch, the Reverend Crumm decided, and with that he gave his whole attention to his visitor.

He did not believe he was ill. What he occasionally said to his more remote parishioners, the sort that did not enter his house, was, 'I need more vim.' One of these had replied not altogether kindly. 'You mean spiritually speaking?' and after careful thought (how hard it is to weigh one's own favourite expressions!) the Reverend Crumm had said, 'No, I don't.' He stood in no detectable danger of losing his faith. His life now was as capable as it had ever been—on the whole it was more capable—of enduring his by no means complacent self-scrutiny. He felt closer to God these days, he spent longer and deeper at his prayers and doing his priestly duty. The usual reply to 'I need more vim', that none of us are getting any younger, also missed the point; he was an athletic fifty four, did all his visiting on foot, played squash most Monday afternoons, preached forcefully, disposed of paper work as swiftly as ever, was polishing an article for *Theology* (if only he had more time for the scholarly side!), had recently joined the Bishop of London's advisory committee on redundant suburban churches. He was in first-rate mental and physical shape. And yet the common thought of advancing years troubled some sleeping part of him. So did a newspaper article he chanced to read, about a group of repatriated prisoners of war from Japan, describing how slow starvation had altered their characters. That was what started him on his vitamin pills. The article maintained that men who are kept short of Vitamin B will turn into liars. Not that the Reverend Crumm had begun telling lies, or experiencing this temptation. He took the pills without locating the impulse of his reasoning. He said he needed more vim.

Unconnected with the pills, as far as he knew, he did not read his favourite poets any more, the glory and the dream made him sad. Something newly ordinary was disturbing him in life and specially in death; and hence, when passing years and changing characters were brought to mind, his sense of getting warmer as he hunted the thimble of his own disquiet. Everything should matter more as dying drew every day one day nearer; he ought to grow both in delight at the unfolding gift of life and in passion to see God: this thought had braced the Reverend Crumm's imagination when he was young, against the far-off time which was now. And now was fortunate but not marvellous. It was not dreadful. He spoke of 'my blessings' like a child remembering its manners. He walked a lot, particularly at night, and strove to give his thoughts of Eternity a mystical twist, while in conversation he made increasing cheery reference to being under the sod. It even occurred to him to wish that God would push off for a while and give him a good fright.

That last fancy he dismissed at once with an inward chuckle, but it returned often, to be dismissed again. Naturally it was not the sort of thing he gave voice to, and on the one occasion he did more or less utter it he awarded himself a black mark. That was only ten days ago, on the Friday, the day young Hammond had presumably come to talk about. He gathered that Gedge was back in hospital. Not surprising. You could see he was hanging by a thread, mentally speaking, the whole of that day.

And all that night too! Great Scott! The Reverend Crumm recalled how Gedge sat in his socks and refused to lie down on the study settee, in this very room, reading passages from his book and explaining what he was going to talk about in Hyde Park the next afternoon.

A fellow like Gedge could end by sending one off the rails oneself.

The front door banged distantly.

A woman entered the room, plainly the lady of the house, and Henry Hammond stopped talking.

'I'm sorry, Leo,' she said, coming on.

Her husband introduced them.

'I didn't know you were busy.'

She sat down.

'Oh Gwen!' he answered her, falsely loud as marriage often is in front of strangers. 'Before we go any further you must be put wise, as our American cousins say. Mr. Hammond has come about that difficult case. My sermon. The disturbance at matins. You will remember. Most difficult. Mr. Hammond wants to discuss the affair and I don't mind admitting—'

'Does he?'

She observed Henry Hammond.

'I only hope Mr. Hammond hasn't been lending him money.' She met her husband's eye and added 'Too.'

'Rest assured,' said Henry Hammond, 'I am a publisher by trade, and publishing is a hard school in such matters.'

The Reverend Crumm followed on at once. 'In any case we are by no means sure that the debt, the small debt incurred towards me, will not be repaid when Gedge finds himself in funds.'

'Finds himself in funds! He is a lunatic. I have heard you say so yourself.'

'Even lunatics must be given the benefit of the doubt, pastorally speaking.'

'That's a benefit I shall pass on as soon as my tradesmen start giving it to me.'

She looked towards Henry Hammond and stated in a sort of undertone, 'I pay the bills.'

'It's all very difficult, my dear,' the Reverend Crumm said.

He too spoke softly; and Henry Hammond, who understood that the exchange was over, now continued with his story. He described his life as a publisher, the arrival of the tortoise, his dealings with Mr. Gedge and Dr. Hennessy. Then he came to last week's supper at Long Acre. He explained he had been invited by Anne Trematon. He did not give her name but referred to her (addressing himself particularly to Mrs. Crumm) as a girl who meant a great deal to him. She too was in publishing, he said, and she like him was worried about the poor madman. He did not mention David at all.

Listening, one would suppose he had known Anne a long time.

'We—she and I—are hatching a plot. Or if that sounds too conspiratorial, we have put our heads together over Gedge and his future. His health, of course, primarily. Suitable occupation must be found for him when he leaves hospital. We think it can be done, it's a great advantage both being in the same walk of life. So you may well ask, sir, where you come in.'

'Goodness me,' said the Reverend Crumm, speaking with emotion, 'my dear chap, I hope I shall never ask any such thing. Any priest worth his salt—'

Mrs. Crumm interposed, 'Naturally we are ready to help, and the question simply is how. Being sentimental won't do any good. Nor will arguing far into the night.'

'Quite so,' said her husband, and, picking up a poker to prod the fire, he muttered something about many mansions.

He did prod.

'A fellow like that!' he then said.

8

Busy though he was, he had joined the Hendon Bird-watchers. Therefore lunch was early.

Mrs. Crumm asked, 'I suppose you'll walk?'

Indicating an ever-present threat, a joke of a threat, he bent his napkin to the line of his waist and answered 'Certainly.'

'The garden keeps *me* fit,' she said. 'And the house.'

Silence fell.

The Reverend Crumm looked out of the window and remarked to his wife the daffodils.

Abruptly, as though the flowers had set her off, she pronounced, 'Did that young man really think we were going to turn ourselves into a mental home?'

'A *convalescent* home, if we are going to talk like that.'

'In these days without servants.'

'A place where the fellow can be sure of a welcome.'

'And borrow money.'

'When he comes out of hospital—' the Reverend Crumm began, but stopped. Steady play! he thought. He was always cautioning himself against being too intellectual. *Convalescent* was not meant to be clever-clever, but it was the sort of thing that got them off on the wrong foot, Gwen and him.

He could not imagine Jesus saying it. But Saint Paul, preaching...? Smiling at this notion, 'I must be off, my dear,' he said, and watched his grey head and thin black body rise in the sideboard mirror opposite. He did look intellectual, he thought, as he turned aside to kiss his wife, telling her not to overdo it. He noted how big the room was, and tall, for just two. And he counted his knuckles on the chairback, his sugar mice the Mater used to call them. A good way to start arithmetic. Candlelight knuckles. Long, long ago.

Is he missing the children? Mrs. Crumm asked herself. She was upstairs. She had removed her skirt and shoes and stockings and was sitting on the bed dangling her legs like a girl.

She wished she could get inside his head.

First things first, was her motto; and, Don't exaggerate. He had become more inward-turning. It was as simple as that.

She put on her gardening trousers. A sudden inspiration, tinged with guilt, made her reach for a pair of his socks. She formulated very firmly: I don't distrust him in any way. She was contemplating his endless half-reasons and crossed reasons for what he did, and she refused to complicate what was simple.

Or should be. She felt sad thinking their prayers together very last thing, after cocoa, had grown embarrassing. They never used to be, and yet he was altogether less passionate now—and even Mrs. Crumm doubted, just here, for a moment, if she made sense to herself. She felt sad for the early days and imagined his clear shape striding along.

Now.

Nobody can keep up.

Is he unhappy?

That's just it, he has become so inward-turning one cannot be certain, it's as simple as that.

'*Solvitur ambulando*. I do my best thinking on my pins.' What the Reverend Crumm told his acquaintances may have been as true as his conviction. Walking was his favourite method of developing the spiritual side, and of fostering sermons, articles, parish policies—and coming to grips with personal problems, like now.

Not very personal in this case because there was no

92

question of having Gedge to stay at the Rectory. Despite young Hammond, despite his own inclinations for that matter, the plan must be scrapped. A couple of minutes walking decided that. Gwen had put her foot down. She hadn't said anything decisive but he could read the signs. And so, instead of wasting time reassembling the arguments, he made a mental list of persons who might be approached with a view to taking in a difficult lodger. The poor chap might be as right as rain when he left hospital. But it was only fair to warn people.

He thought of five names and left it there. A safe margin. One of those five would turn up trumps. And Gedge, once settled, would find companionship in the parish, for example at the Wednesday evening discussions. Though he would need firm handling.

Good, the Reverend Crumm concluded. He foresaw one of those taxing relationships which can be so worthwhile.

Next he reminded himself it was spring, and where he was going. God's world. He must keep his ears open and not neglect his birdsong drill. He walked on and on, between Finchley and Hendon, long raking strides. Thrushes everywhere it seemed. He mimicked the invisible birds in his head, but he was not entirely at ease, the idea of firm handling had sent him back to Gedge's talk of holding hands among many other things during that unending Friday night, and then there was the money problem, the loan, the debt, and the prospect of Gedge not to stay of course but even visiting the Rectory. He walked on. Sufficient unto the day: he challenged his hot mantling sensation with a resolve to look carefully at the next interesting tree.

God's world.

He had to wait for his tree, the gardens were small here with low repressed hedges. He hummed and practised patience and eventually, in an open space where a garage was beginning to be built, he came upon a young beech. He recognised its kind by the trunk and then by the leaves in bud.

He drew a branch to him and studied the supple tracery, moving his fingers along and outward to the tight slim furls, the laughably sharp pencils of brown. Not sticky, he noted, taking one, pinching, rolling. And, bending close to it, no scent. He stepped back, his mind on the Creator of all, to survey the whole tree. The other side—the south side, he knowingly observed—was ahead and showing the true and tender green. He was about to inspect the baby leaves when a man emerged from the house next to the garage and said good afternoon. They chatted. The Reverend Crumm reached for a branch and quoted 'Beechen green,' dandling it between them, 'Beechen green and shadows numberless'. He asked the man if he knew the *Ode to a Nightingale*. The man said he did, but this was a copper beech.

I call it a revelation! thought the Reverend Crumm, pulling his nose every few yards as he continued his walk alone. God had caught him napping. He (Lionel Crumm) knew a beech when he saw one, but he had spent fifty-four years on this planet without noticing copper beeches begin green each spring and change colour through the summer.

He stopped.

Something else had occurred to him.

Like robins turning scarlet in midwinter.

The comparison thrust him higher still, exalted him unspeakably. By jove! he thought, words are no good! It was far from nonsense what he had been saying recently about needing more vim. If you ignored the words. So he walked even more briskly than before until he came to a telephone kiosk. Then he paused in its shadow.

He offered God back the greatness and variety of life, steering clear of words as far as possible. Not easy. He strove to empty his mind which persisted in lying before him in hazy splendour; it was too much his. Something that felt less his, a light-blue jellyfish shape floated past his closed eyes. God's world. While he was following the jellyfish it burst into stars. The stars turned pink and danced. He stroked both eyelids to quieten his sealed vision, and again, and again, for peace, for God. But a bird's song pierced his ear, one he did not know. He puzzled to identify it, then checked his erring course and said the Lord's prayer, words admittedly, nevertheless on the right lines.

The remainder of his walk to Hendon was businesslike. He used the copper beech to block in an important section of his sermon for the Sunday after next. *Christ and Hiroshima.* The notice board ran a month ahead, so he was committed to this title. Advertise or perish.

He had already determined to preach a sermon of dramatic contrast: Love and Life against Hatred and Death, and (the time being April) he had planned to develop, literally and metaphorically, and with a scientific and genetic aspect too, the Threat of Sterility. He would range from modern art to animal reproduction. To keep them on their toes, instead of beginning with the miracle of spring he intended to examine the biological implications of the atom bomb. These facts must be faced and stated. 'Knowledge cannot hurt the truth' he was going to exclaim, rather loud, as if impromptu, 'even in 1947.'

So far so good. But how to work the transition from negative to positive, from Hiroshima to Our Lord?

By simple anecdote, he now saw. He would tell them about the beech tree. With delight he understood that this little story against himself could be made to serve a spiritual purpose; for the sermon was really a counter-attack on the scientific mentality, indeed on all forms of intellectual pride and complacency; he had not recognised this clearly before, but that was what it was; and the most insidious pride and complacency is the presuming to know God's creative purpose. Copper beech and robin redbreast. 'Nature is witty,' somebody once said. The divine wisdom includes wit. I thought I knew what He was up to, thought the Reverend Crumm.

For quite three minutes he basked in a large prosperity of

paradox. His own admiring, even devout attitude to new life had proved himself less than fully alive. The Threat of Sterility. He cupped his hands together as he walked. He had 'got' his sermon. Half an hour at Dreadnought the old typewriter would see it through.

Publishable perhaps?

He looked at his watch and registered, I must walk like smoke—mixed up with which, How good God is! A clairvoyance of love was spreading outward from the copper beech and the sermon. It even came to him who had said 'Nature is witty.'

His stomach rumbled. He actually felt hungry and thought about dying and going elsewhere, and then, fortified, he returned to the Gedge question. For the first time he looked straight at its embarrassment. He told himself a truth: it was rot to pretend he was seriously worried about Friday night. Wild things were said then on both sides, in the tussle, but he (as always) was putting the religious case dramatically, and Gedge poor fellow was *non compos*. No, be honest, what troubled him was not the memory of Friday but having committed himself morally speaking to more discussions like it.

Why? he asked, it's my duty that sort of thing.

He walked and thought until he located the reason at home, and then he affirmed I don't like dealing with ultimates at the Rectory.

He asked again, with rare persistence, why? He meant why mind *that* when the world is full of tragedy.

By now he was at a limit, against a wall of his nature, but it felt like moving forward as he named conditions in which to talk of the deepest things came easily to him, anyhow fittingly. Visits to schools. Running into old friends —the surprise. Some pubs. Houses of grief, one left it to God then. The pulpit in a way. Only in a way.

The conference table. Sober. Objective. It's rum, thought he, it hadn't occurred to him before but it *was* strange, the urge to make profound but personal remarks there, the energy they released, almost a vulgar thrill, bright comet's tail of private deposition sauced with ultimates. He recalled pen trays and poised quiescent heads and himself addressing a concourse of virtual strangers on marriage and the priestly vocation. Like young joy, it felt. Exhibitionism! he had warned himself. Chin in! guard up! Then, 'If I may conclude with a few observations from within the strait-jacket, strait and narrow jacket,' pause for smiles, 'the mystic freedom,' pause for thought, 'the joys and sorrows of Christian wedlock,'—and on to the God-given tasks ('four hands are better than two'), the joint self-denials including qualified celibacy was his phrase, and never forget the glorious privileges. In fact he ended with the glory and the dream. Tainted perhaps but strong—then who are the pure in heart if you think—whereas his words had turned poor and awkward when he got home, and weary, under-lining I need more vim, and Gwen received the merest loving sketch.

My wires are crossed, he tersely decided, for his walk's end was in sight, Hendon Secondary Modern School, brand new post-war, the Science Block, green roof, optimistic windows and the biology master, good man, their president, inside by now with epidiascope and slides, and today the wagtail family.

Crossed wires. It was simply his experience that uncrossed ones are better. They keep a chap's spiritual powder dry. At least they help to.

Reticence is in itself no vice, he suddenly thought.

But if Gedge was going to appear (and he was) at the Rectory, and Gwen to and fro popping in and bound to hear ends and beginnings, as she had every right, then she must be told certain things at once.

Well, soon.

What things?

The remarkable fact, as he entered the school gates, was that more of these Gedge situations had not arisen over the years. In a way they had, but nearly always one could meet people on their own ground. And so it would have been with Gedge, probably, depending on his lodgings. But the two of them had discovered some time in the middle of Friday night that they both believed in physical exercise. They shook hands impulsively upon their accord. '*Solvitur ambulando.*' 'Those marching legions!' replied Gedge who seemed to find the Latin tag amusing. 'Part of the fun will be walking here,' Gedge then said, 'and after hospital, just won't I be tired. I will want to argue lying down while you pace the quarter-deck.' Caught napping, the Reverend Crumm had not the heart to say no.

What things must Gwen be told?

The Reverend Crumm climbed the deserted staircase of the Science Block, and decided: enough to put her in the picture. It need not be much, she had heard young Hammond's story. In the next day or two, anyhow soon he would say a bit more about the money side, the loan. Details weren't important, the exact figure didn't matter, peace was what mattered. In any case it was only ten pounds. Then there was the question of Gedge's lodgings. And he ought to mention the pale young man, a boy really, even younger than Hammond, who also appeared to be a friend of Gedge's. Rather unhealthy if you thought about it. The discrepancy in age. He would just mention the pale boy who gave no name and buttonholed him in the porch after evensong. It would fit in quite naturally. And eventually Gedge would come. To talk. And as for my dislike of ultimates at the Rectory, I must lump that, thought the Reverend Crumm.

9

THE other side of London, Anne Trematon was remaking her brother's bed. She guessed that he had begun to sleep badly. That was all she knew.

She was alone in the flat, spending her lunch-break here.

Yes, she said to herself, a dog-basket, look. The bottom sheet was wrinkled and bitty, worse than she suspected. She drew it tight and brushed it. Then she attended to his pillow. It was not the right day, but she gave him clean pyjamas. During the final smoothing and tucking a finger got scratched on a loose wire underneath. It was nothing.

Early afternoons, this time of year, the sun caught his window a glancing keen stroke but scarcely shone in. Anne took her finger to the window. While she was regarding it one prick of blood appeared at the deeper end of the furrow. It stood so small and round and dark and, now it had come, so momentously still and faithful to the laws of the world, so itself, that she reached for her handkerchief with a fulfilled, impersonal sensation, and stood there dreaming, still looking at the blood. Until something prompted her, and she turned and surveyed David's room in its silence and complete daytime suspension, the clothes and ornaments and three or four trophies, everything with its known history. The signs of work and aspiration touched her in her present anxiety for him. She did a thing she had never done before. Wrapping her handkerchief round the white scratch, she thrust her arm down inside his bed and wished.

Her little brother.

He always wanted the moon.

She must go back to work, but first it was worth checking that the Handel sonata had gone. She would like to be sure he was doing what he said he was going to do. If Wack had been on the phone she would have rung him up now and casually asked, 'is David there?'

The Handel sonata had gone. That proved nothing but it was a comfort. As she set off for the office she felt happy and sad at the same time, remembering their parting words. 'It's very easy,' he had said about the Handel; and he went on at once in his frowning way, 'but nothing is easy to play well,' as if she did not know this. 'Why are you and Wack playing it?' 'Studying it,' he corrected her. 'Studying it, David?' 'There are some problems of tone production. Actually, tone *projection*. Handel is what we need, he is so broad and dramatic, in some moods Beethoven believed he was an even greater master than Bach.'

But she did not like the look in his eyes.

10

ANNE also found cause for alarm in his new habit of smiling with the muscles of his mouth. This smile came from nowhere and failed to possess his face. It came when he rattled Wack's letter-box. He was bracing himself for their meeting.

'Handel!' said David.

'Handel!' replied Wack. 'This is well known.' Which meant there was a clear agreement. An agreement to play Handel. David had suggested it the day before without any explanation, so he now started to talk, in the doorway and climbing the stairs, almost gabbling.

Wack cut him short by half stating: surely it was the G minor double violin sonata David had in mind—'and who is going to lead?'

'I thought I would,' said David, 'that is really the point,' and he began his story again sitting upstairs under Wack's abstracted and, he felt, faintly mistrustful surveillance. Wack kept doing small tasks about the room. He was wearing his green silk dressing-gown. The metal side grips of his trousers were undone, and when he moved they tinkled. He excused himself in the middle of things and David heard him washing and cleaning his teeth behind the screen. Then he emerged patting his hands softly on a towel, and said 'Continue please.'

David was explaining that he felt worried about work. He had noticed his concentration wandering recently—not in the quartet, not yet anyhow, but on his own. And connected with this, in the evenings, while he practised at home, he had caught himself folding his wings, stroking his inner ear like an amateur, instead of throwing out his sound and placing it for judgment.

He described how it was. When he got so far he began to fumble and repeat. It was difficult to say more without bringing in the rest of his life. 'It's not real,' he remarked, 'not music, turning to yourself like that, playing inwards, it is a sort of consolation.' Wack's mouth was open ready to reply, and David added 'But music does console people of course. In their lives I mean.' Next, to his own disquiet, for he did not see himself like this, and he was under increasing strain today and for several days: 'Music is my religion.'

'It is the English fault.'

'What do you mean?'

'This weak dreaming. It seems sufficient for poems. And for cricket, Hans Neumann has said to me.'

'You know it has never been true of me.'

'Never. Absolutely. But a fault may show itself.'

The possibility confronted David in the form of an unexpected yet somehow dreaded guest. He received it while Wack picked up the printed music he had brought, the double sonata, and, standing stiff-backed, said, 'Handel. Yes. I am thinking of the English composers. Handel. And his enemy—rival you say—Buononcini. And Johann Christian, the English Bach. And Haydn who earned money in England. And the poor Mendelssohn.'

'Purcell was an Englishman.'

It was as if somebody else had spoken, so much so that David wondered: is this the exact moment of what will be called a breakdown, or going mad even? He tested in his head 'Purcell was an Englishman' to try and own it. Then he realised his thoughts were wrong too. He was used to being teased by Wack and Hans Neumann about England and English music, everything English. He did not mind, he always laughed, he was proud, he loved it when Wack called Anne 'Flower of London', though this was also a sort of teasing. It was a joke at least. Was it kind? He had never considered.

Wack appeared to have noticed something, for he asked David if he was having trouble with his ears.

David assured him not, but seized the opportunity to mention his indigestion, he supposed that was what it was, and how his fingers were sticky with sweat often. They had never sweated before. He was hesitating whether to say anything about his sleep, wherever that might lead them. It felt more personal than his stomach and fingers.

'Nevertheless,' said Wack with a fending-off gesture, 'I will not arg you, I will advise you to buy, from a merchant in Victoria Street, near to here'—he retired once more behind his screen and came out with a small box, a stud box or jewel case—'these ones.' Inside the box was a pair of rubber plugs. 'Like this,' he said, and stuffed them in his ears.

'What are they for?'

'You say?' He was pulling them out again.

'What for?'

'For three shillings only and some pennies.'

'What good do they do your ears?'

'They prevent all pressures of the air. I wear my stops on the underground train.'

'But I never go by tube, as you know.'

'Elsewhere we find these pressures.'

That remote royal certainty drove David away. And the horrible plugs. He could not bear Handel and decided then and there, I am a case for the doctor. He left his violin behind and went away, saying he was unwell, determining to walk and keep to the main roads. They presented the best chance of arriving if it grew dark in his head. He wrapped all his fears in one surrender, and suffered less, immediately.

11

Dr. Hennessy was sitting apart quite by himself in a place called Medical Staff Common Room. A cup of tea rested on the arm of his chair.

'Hullo, hullo, hullo. It's you. Well, you have caught the profession with its feet up,' he said, turning back to his newspaper. 'Listen to this.'

He looked younger than David remembered.

He read aloud quietly but with relish.

It was the story of a child changing its sex. It lived in a house called Bide-a-bit which, so the reporter said, was like the other houses in that street. The parents were ordinary too, according to the reporter. They said they were naturally thrilled but it took getting used to. The little boy's name was Leslie. He had been Lesley before. The reporter told the family that the whole nation had taken them to its heart, and he asked Leslie how he felt. Leslie said boys were the teachers' favourites at his school. The reporter then talked to him about what he wanted to do when he grew up. Leslie named some things he did not want to do. It was a long list. Dr. Hennessy gave up in the middle and asked David, 'And what can I do for you?'

'Not here,' David said.

'Then we'll find a corner. No hurry. Have a cup of tea first. It's on the house. It will be on all of us when the Health Service gets started. You and Leslie and the rest had better hurry up with your careers, the country will need more taxpayers.'

David refused tea.

They went to the little office opposite Alamein Ward. All seemed quiet.

'Now tell me,' said Dr. Hennessy as he shut the door.

David burst into tears.

'You thought you weren't, but in fact you are going to have some tea,' Dr. Hennessy said. 'Sit down there—no there—a minute while I fetch it.'

Opening a folder with various papers inside, Dr. Hennessy said 'Let me see.'

'It was eleven days ago. At night. About ten o'clock. I was outside the door of Alamein Ward and you came up behind me. It will be a fortnight on Sunday. I don't know if you remember.'

'How can I forget?' was the reply, not sarcastic or anything else very much because the doctor was still shuffling through his papers. 'Hold on while I get myself up to date. A lot has happened on the medical front in the last eleven days. Let me see. There is nothing about you here,' he added as an afterthought.

'No,' said David.

'This is all Gedge.'

'Yes,' said David.

'In due course I am going to ask you why you think you are ill or mad or whatever. But just now it would be a good idea to concentrate on Gedge.'

'Yes,' said David. He was trying to mean yes, completely yes, to both the due course and the just now.

'Take a few minutes holiday from yourself and think about Gedge.'

'Yes,' said David.

'With him it's not a question of supposing, he really is ill.'

'Yes,' said David.

He was determined to co-operate.

'And I dreamt—'

'You had had a bit to drink that first night.'

'Yes.'

'Go on.'

'I dreamt I was standing by his cot. Everything was like it had been earlier except I knew he was dead.'

'How did you know?'

'He was smooth and the smell had gone. I rang a bell. It was broken but you came in all the same. I told you he had turned to stone. I was glad in my dream. You said "No, it's one of these new synthetics," and you rubbed your hand over his face to prove it. Someone was folding his blankets. I remember asking "How will he ever get warm?" and you said "Keep the party clean" because Sister Osborne was there too.'

'So you would call it a happy dream.'

'He was dead.'

'But you were glad.'

'In my dream. I woke up then and never went to sleep again, and the next night I lay awake until it was morning, it was light when I dropped off, and when my sister came in to wake me I was dreaming of her and me on a big lawn waiting to be presented to the King.'

'That was Monday.'

'Yes.'

'Your second bad night. I'm getting this sorted out gradually. Therefore it was the third night, Tuesday, that you got out of bed and made a bonfire of Gedge's hat. In retrospect you consider this was a mad thing to do. Why?'

12

Insomnia was the great exception in David's life, because changes, new things, tended to happen to him gradually, like over Bidder and Son south of the river.

He walked past the shop most days through the fifties and early sixties. The first time he stopped was a dark winter morning and their lights were still on. The complete bodies on hooks appeased him, and he was intrigued by the weeping snouts. He took to stopping. He rarely bought anything, as a rule he looked through the door and away again. Bidder used to twinkle his knife in greeting.

Often the Son was scattering sawdust. He swept it up last thing in the evening, and during the day made quiet brown mounds of mince and held plucked birds over a flame for singeing. It seemed he was also given certain exacting tasks. He removed ribs nigglingly from sides of bacon. On occasion David saw him bent low over a single great dumb-bell of bone. Mrs. Bidder made up the parcels. The Son drove the van.

First they altered 'Purveyor of High Class Meat' to 'Family Butcher', then they added 'Continental Specialities', and later again 'Deliveries' was painted out. The sawdust disappeared; a hose was used at weekends instead. At about the same time as the hose the shop itself was divided into two halves, and from now on the Son stood behind a delicatessen counter wearing a chef's hat. He also minded the deep freeze when it arrived. His side was where the marble slab had been, the place for prepared joints to stand until the van was ready, trussed or skewered beef on grease-proof paper, and legs of mutton with snapped shanks, and all shapes of pork to whose skin, nearly hairless skin,

Mr. Bidder dealt slashing contours like tribal scars; and against these moist surfaces of meat Mrs. Bidder used to press her tickets. A conference was sometimes called before she wrapped a parcel finally from view. Her favourite remark was 'All right then?' She used it to her husband about anything in the shop and also asking customers how they were. When deliveries stopped she worked at another place in the mornings, and otherwise she helped with the till which stayed remarkably the same. But garlic sausages hung on the hooks where the carcases had been, joints became fewer, meat was chopped abruptly into thawing edgy shapes in trays in the window. The trays were decorated with parsley and little slogans of commendation. One day, walking home from work, David noticed something amiss with the parsley. He approached closer and saw it had become plastic overnight: at which moment a heavy lorry stopped in the street behind his back with a *tush* then a *tush tush* of air brakes, and he was set thinking about the last fifteen years. He entered and bought a chop from Mr. Bidder, and threw it away, burnt it, still wrapped, as soon as he got home.

But when Dr. Hennessy asked him 'Are you in the habit of burning things?' his answer then was 'No.' If it had been a habit he might have felt less afraid.

'No,' he repeated.

'The burning urge is not uncommon, you know. We recognise it. The word is pyromania. But tell me, laddie.' Dr. Hennessy moved sharply in his chair as if to say the best of jokes must end. 'You plainly did not go to bed on Tuesday night intending to cremate Gedge's hat. Did you? Surely not. What started you on that tack?'

'I got the idea,' said David, 'that he had stolen my sleep. I mean I thought he needed it to finish his book, my sleep as well as his own, I felt as if I was on a mountain top with him. You can see it's mad but Tuesday was the third night. I'm getting used to it now.'

'To having mad ideas or to not sleeping?'

'I don't know. The two things get mixed up.'

'Then I suggest we unmix them and leave madness out of it.'

David tried to. He described brewing a hot milky drink according to the advertisements, and picking up a dull book before bed. Dr. Hennessy was encouraging and said there was no hurry. He sat at his desk while the net curtains puffed and fell straight behind him at the whim of the air, and all noises sounded far away. 'What book was that?' he asked. 'Don't be shy about details.' David assured him 'I'm not'—and he omitted nothing except saying his prayers, a practice which had lapsed for some years, and asking for a night's sleep. He described what was in his mind as exactly as he could remember, and how his panic grew. Dr. Hennessy asked him to be as precise as possible. Because there were many kinds of panic. David agreed and explained that already by bedtime on Tuesday he was dreading another day not separate from the one before. He longed for a new morning, just a new one, it needn't be nice. Otherwise even his music was beginning to go badly. Dr. Hennessy said, 'Your music is bound to go badly sometimes, however much you sleep. That's life.' David agreed again, but talked about the other sort of going badly, no matter how badly, where a thing remained really completely hopeful. 'I see,' said Dr. Hennessy, 'and tell me about your sister's bedtime routine.'

Anne liked reading detective stories and books by the Sitwells. Her light could be seen under the door, it was part of falling asleep, for David. When he woke from his dream of Mr. Gedge being dead on Sunday night her light was still on, so the time could not be much after midnight. It went out soon after that. For the first time in his life he saw it go out and heard the click of her light-switch.

And again on Monday. Waiting for it on Tuesday had a lot to do with his panic, and when it happened he felt not so bad because it had happened, and he climbed out of bed to tighten his pyjama cord. There was a moon. He crossed towards the window presumably to look at the moon, he couldn't be sure now, he never reached the window.

'I trod on it.'

'I'm with you,' said Dr. Hennessy.

'I trod on it.'

'Quite so. With bare feet.'

'I touched it with one foot, just the brim.'

'But enough to get you worrying about—contagion.'

'Not really.'

'Then tell me.'

'It reminded me of Mr. Gedge.'

'Of course.'

'How he was in Hyde Park, everything, the ladder, the book, his gloves.'

'That's what I mean,' Dr. Hennessy said. 'And three hours later, when you burnt the hat, when you took it down to this old stove in your basement, how did you carry it?'

'Between two coat-hangers.'

They regarded each other for quite a minute.

'See?' said Dr. Hennessy.

13

'AND now I'm going to give you some advice, though I
don't expect you will take it.'

Why not? David wondered. It struck new dread through
him that scientifically, to the medical judgment, he was not
likely to accept advice, after coming here, at the end of a
long afternoon's truthful talk.

Dr. Hennessy continued, 'Find somewhere on your own
to live.'

He was still sitting at his desk in the little office opposite
Alamein Ward, the window wide open behind him and
net curtains blowing. What had he said? I don't know, I
came for help, David thought, how bad things must be if
I'm expected to reject the help I get. He had been listening
carefully so far, but not now, though he sat very still. The
walls of his heart seemed to be collapsing inward. Dr. Hennessy was about to speak again. One could tell.

'It is time you stopped sharing with your sister.'

David stared at him. He half understood. 'I don't understand,' he said.

'I will explain.'

Dr. Hennessy tilted back in his chair to collect his
thoughts.

In a confused rush David recalled: and he knows nothing
about Henry Hammond.

He tilted backwards, his eyes raised, deliberately, but for
some reason looked down in the middle of this process and
added, 'I'm not saying you should see nothing of her.' And
then he changed his mind altogether. 'You are a nice kid,'
he suddenly declared. He was observing David with close
attention. It was obvious he was not going to explain any-

thing just now. He untilted his chair. Still watching David, he pulled open a drawer of his desk and took out some paper. He wrote.

When he had finished he asked, 'Have you a family doctor?' David told him no. 'Then I'm not only on the right side of the law,' he said, 'I'm even being ethical.' The last notion amused him. He handed the paper across. 'This is a prescription for a mild sedative, to tide you over the next few days and help you sleep. One spoonful after meals. It will tell you on the label. Don't be afraid of taking two spoonfuls if one doesn't work. You won't kill yourself if you drink the lot. But it would be a bad idea.'

David thanked him and got up to go.

'What about this indigestion of yours?' Dr. Hennessy asked. 'Hop up on to the couch and loosen your trousers.'

Flat as flat.

'Head back laddie ... relax ... there.'

Peace.

His final probe was to lay the side of a cool hand high under the ribs, on the right, and press. 'Tender I expect.' 'Yes,' said David, 'only tender.' He had not known such peace for days. He noticed Dr. Hennessy had had his hair cut. The fear of a minute ago, where had it gone? 'No fell disease,' said Dr. Hennessy, 'that I can detect. But you need to be sensible. People like you can end up with an ulcer. Or more than one. Did you see what President Truman said the other day to a journalist who had been rude about his daughter's singing? "You're an eight ulcer man on four ulcer pay." What a country!'

David was lifted on a swell of confidence to say that indigestion was not really a good description. 'It is more like feeling sick. A bit sick and full. Like too much fat. It is like carrying a dead fish under your ribs.'

'I know the kind,' Dr. Hennessy said at once, in evident satisfaction. 'Very dead and bluey-white underneath. I always tell folk they are suffering from mental indigestion, but I prefer your resident fish.'

Then David asked, 'What shall I do when the medicine is finished?'

'I'm at your service. What do you suggest?'

'What do *you* suggest?'

He enjoyed being bold. The change was extraordinary. Without forming any idea of it beyond his own pertness, he began to enjoy the whole situation. It was pleasant getting tidy and ready to go, with a sense of leisure at last. He also enjoyed making the actual appointment. It stood in the big Engagements Book binding him to return in ten days— 'at an hour that suits your work and mine,' Dr. Hennessy very politely said, but also teasing him.

However to sit at home and remember was not enjoyable. If he failed to understand before—and did he fail?—he could not help flinching now from the touch that had been laid upon his life with Anne. Dr. Hennessy did not mention it again, the subject should have died, a better time had followed and it should have been carried down the stream somewhere. But it was still in the offing. David stood aside helplessly, himself at the hospital in his present mind's eye, while his time there got shaken up and restated like a box of dice.

He was not afraid. The meaning he read now was not the old shape of fear. He was at the kitchen table, manuscript sheet-music spread over the table in front of him. Anne would be back soon. He ought to be copying, he was home. He had fetched his violin on the way back from the hospital, where Wack showed no surprise, they even played a movement of the Handel, so much can happen in one afternoon.

He ought to be copying.

Actually his eyes wandered round the kitchen. He was imagining living in some other place.

Even so, though not happy, he was not afraid. His recent boldness stayed with him while the kitchen and the passing minutes marshalled it towards a carping, theoretical gratitude. He doesn't realise how much he has done for me, or (to be more exact) how little there was to do, he told himself about Dr. Hennessy, because after all he was not ill, he only needed telling that. And from there he moved forward to question the other diagnostic touch, the one he flinched from. In the end probably (he conceded), well almost certainly, we will live apart. Life is like that, he grandly posed; and then, What must be must be—assuming the words, trying them on for size from his small heroic wardrobe, while determination hardened as regards what need not be now. He would never forget to be grateful. The medicine would be ready before the chemist shut tonight. Sleep and work and home. Gratitude was one thing, but seeing the whole world with Dr. Hennessy's eyes was quite another.

The low whining pulse of the fridge cut in upon the silent room. David glanced at the light, the two-way switch, in mind of Henry Hammond, Anne's ice cream, Wack, the four of them clustered round that sweet white wine. He smiled at an amusing joyless idea. *Hennessy* and *Hammond* and Mr. Gedge is *Henry* too and I have just been playing *Handel*, it's as if somebody had made it all up, David thought. It was like a baby's dream, not the blue and white sort, an evil dream. He ought to be copying music. Still smiling, he opened the drawer of the kitchen table and began to play with their potato peeler, by feel, the lancet slit, so very known and used and used and used; and he looked about him and imagined.

Leave home! That showed complete failure to understand how he and Anne were. In these circumstances David must be his own master and know what part to reject, when to say no. The folly of it—leave home!—proved Dr. Hennessy's skill had deserted him, well not him—David had got back peace virtually and was grateful—not him but one area, one province of his care (and so it should with this part coming right) and had settled on Mr. Gedge who needed it all, all the skill, the medical knowledge, the more than skill—call it by its right name—the wisdom which made Dr. Hennessy say, 'Take a holiday from yourself and think about Gedge, with him it's not a question of supposing, he really is ill.' Mr. Gedge's case is separate. Leave home! is a funny way of saying it won't affect him whatever I do. No wonder Dr. Hennessy didn't expect me to take his advice. And eleven days ago—I hated it at the time—he said 'I wouldn't have him home if I were you.' Well he's not me, I'm me, and I'm not surprised he wants to get on with curing Mr. Gedge and thinks of me and Mr. Gedge as completely separate, so much so that I couldn't make him really interested in why I burnt Mr. Gedge's hat, I kept on returning to it and in the end he said 'There's too much popularised Freud around nowadays,' and I avoided the word mad and said, 'But it was an extraordinary thing to do,' and he said, 'Not at all. You were frightened. You had to pick on something, this was your third bad night running. Everything seems worse at night. It's not as if you were a veteran insomniac,' and then he looked more serious and said, 'You mustn't fuss. Human beings have had fantasies about defilement since the beginning of time. Laddie, there's no harm believing madness to be infectious, but remember sanity is catching too. I mean it. You must relax. You *are* tense aren't you. Be sensible and you'll do fine. What's a burnt hat between friends? Now if your fear of defilement had taken a different form, if for example you had sprung an urge to wash your hands every few minutes, that might be serious,' and I said, 'And what about wearing gloves all the time?' and he said, 'Ah yes' because he could see what I was thinking—he said 'Ah yes. But we have other things the matter there as well.'

14

NOWADAYS Henry Hammond averted his eyes from the windows of lingerie shops; falling in love had these marked effects on him. When he joked with girl clerks and typists, it, his whole address, was mild to his perception and Socratic, older than old age, and the pressure of love felt visible on his brow like the lines a wise fate might draw. He dispensed with lunch—in this and other ways he was saving money assiduously. Eating less had spiritual force too, of course. So had his new habit of staying late at the office. When all was quiet he dedicated the work of the day, the future, his best hopes, to his own self and Anne Trematon. It was like knights and vigils, and indeed it had occurred to him once or twice recently that there might be something in Christianity, though he had no idea if she was religious.

He sat in the darkening office staring at the telephone. By himself at last. He was not a 'glorified clerk' as Dr. Hennessy had told David, but it was true he shared a room with two others. He was summoning the will to ring her up. It hurt. He had discovered sorrow. Sorrow was his friend. So was absolute joy. The condition of his heart amazed him, repaying, in his view, more than ever before, the closest scrutiny.

His desk was distinguished by a rather grand paper-knife. This he now placed centrally and spun, and spun again, and again, promising, swearing to himself to start dialling as soon as it came to rest with its point towards the silent black machine. The knife was a good spinner. So he sat and spun diligently. He knew her number; a few days ago he had done this very deed, without the help of spinning, but her bother answered and he now most earnestly wished he had not said 'Sorry, wrong number' before he put the receiver down because his voice was surely recognisable.

And when at last the paper-knife slowed and stopped and pointed so straight at the telephone nobody could deny it, Henry Hammond recalled her face once more. He had not seen her since the supper at Long Acre. Since then, suspecting something unworthy and below his true quality, he had withheld the rest of her from his mind's eye, but not her face. Advisedly through the past fortnight he had fed his passion on her face, and he was encouraging it to graze now, to wander and report to him while he stared at the telephone. For a tiny bubble of spit had a way of forming and maintaining itself in the left—always the left—corner of her mouth while she talked, not that she talked much. Nobody else would have noticed it, it was his bubble, and problematic and obviously frail, yet stubborn in its secret hold on him; it was the very essence of the uncommon-place, and he sat at his desk and proved himself upon it at a height where nobody else would have remarked it even. A mere bubble. No one else. No one.

But for the war he would have gone to Cambridge. He had a scholarship to one of the smaller colleges. Just before leaving the army he made a snap decision to forego his scholarship and enter publishing at once.

Despite the speed, the odds were carefully calculated. When Smith and Nordenfeld offered to make him what they called a trainee editor, he noted the gaps created by time and chance in the human ladder of that firm—the men who had found other jobs or got killed—and at the very top he perceived three ageing directors and an American. The American appeared to like him in interview.

Henry Hammond did some quick reckoning and made his choice. Certainly he was doing well so far. But it was also clear that in one particular direction he had misread the signs. Lacking money and social background, and being young, he overestimated the post-war cachet of his King's commission in a smart regiment. He never quite got the measure of the welcome he received when he joined their uniformed society. The Christian names, the cool solicitude, the fairness. Their equally friendly farewell, again temperate, he could and did encompass, he caught the tone of their goodbye to a temporary comrade in arms, goodbye till the next war, but by now it was too late. While he was stepping out of his full-dress uniform for the last (which was almost the first) time, aged twenty-one, behind a curtain in a photographer's studio, he imagined Cambridge with some pain.

All the more resolutely did he set about making his mark. That same afternoon he posted a manuscript to *Horizon*. By nine o'clock the next morning he had begun a private scheme of study; he sat in a municipal library reading a textbook on the law of copyright, working his way inward (the idea was) from the technical fringe to the heart of his chosen profession. He determined to get there by the time he crossed the threshold of Smith and Nordenfeld's to do his first day's work. And that was what happened. But by then, also, his short story had come back with a letter of rejection from Cyril Connolly himself, in his own hand, praising certain things. Was the letter really encouraging, he wondered, and not just kind? while he fought his disappointment. He decided it was. From photographs Connolly did not look the sort of editor who wrote quite long letters unless he detected talent. So, on the last day of his demobilisation leave, the rejected story was posted to *Penguin New Writing*, and a poem 'On First Seeing the Rhine' went back to *Horizon* with a grateful letter admitting the faults of the story and stressing the anti-romantic intention of the poem. 'Our poor bruised Europe!' he wrote to Connolly. 'What are we to make of it all, we inheritors of this undreamed-of Waste Land? If my verse strikes you as compassionately ironic, in its gropings at least, I shall be well pleased.'

Henry Hammond's was a dying type, and his models were old-fashioned themselves. Often, in the army, he used to watch a particular brigade major eating, drinking, reading the newspapers; he observed his shoes and how he spoke to servants. This major was a wartime soldier like himself. He smelt of something like but not soap. His name was Cazalet. He had established a flourishing practice at the Chancery Bar but had also found time, they said, to write a witty book on Gladstone and his fallen women. Simply by watching Major Cazalet, evening after evening in the mess, Henry Hammond cured himself of various underbred habits such as tucking in his legs so people should not trip over them; he examined all of the major that was not hidden by his newspaper, evening after evening, and pondered Cambridge, and noted that the best gins are pink, and otherwise pruned and manured his future. He pictured the major's life and let it merge with what he knew of other examples; and decided to succeed this way. This way stood, as yet, distantly sublime, and also very copycat. But he should not be judged exceptionally vague or unconfident in his creative plans (though he kept them secret) as opposed to his 'career' which he talked a lot about; indeed how can one be sure that he possessed absolutely no gift? The truth was, his quick wits had a tendency to obscure the issue. This was always so. Back at school, for example, in 1938, he wrote a thunderous poem in free verse on Munich, Hitler, and England's Shame. Inevitably it won pride of place in the magazine of his London grammar school, but when he heard that his poem had been christened 'Murgatroyd' in the masters' common room, he saw the point and never wrote like that again.

One day four years later, not in his own mess, he had been seconded to the Green Howards, he saw a senior officer quite literally toss a book out of the window—a big book.

This was *Ulysses*. Henry Hammond found a copy and decided after reading most of it that he was a prose-writer rather than a poet. Novels need not be like Arnold Bennett, he now realised. And later again he read D. H. Lawrence. Lawrence called Bennett a pig in clover. On the other hand a novel by Lawrence was very unlike *Ulysses*. It should be possible, Henry Hammond decided, to house his own talent in this form.

He located his self-styled originality through a process of close, defensive attention to his brother officers as well as by reading advanced books. When one of them remarked, in that languid way of theirs, that someone or other had disappointing breasts, he concluded that the truth was not being fully told. The balance was wrong. 'Slept with lots of pretty girls?' their kind though fussy adjutant would enquire, and again Henry Hammond was dissatisfied. The harvest of a week's embarkation leave should not, could not be expressed thus. How different every woman feels inside! he urged, calling in aid his own slender experience to challenge such representations. For he had the idea that good writers milk particularities bucketwise into their books; and being by no means precociously vicious, and at the same time and in a normal degree occupied with sex, he held his youth a temporary disadvantage. What scraps he had, he treasured: an ugly mark, almost raw, caused by a safety pin because the more expensive ones have to keep their stockings up somehow when their suspenders break; and another with black hair but not true black but dirty, greasy, hiding its fire—and between her legs, a golden fleece. These were facts. He recorded them in his notebook. They seemed dependable. And in default of experience he promoted his fantasies, the more grotesque the better because (he supposed) what is grotesque cannot be entirely commonplace. He had a recurring dream about living with a leopard. Also, older women set him off. When he called on the Reverend Crumm and Mrs. Crumm interrupted their talk, he scarcely noticed her at first. But he watched her from behind while she was leaving the room and his thought of the wife exploded into a mental measuring of the pints and pints—gallons with average luck—of male fluid she must have taken aboard over the years.

To be involuntary and by those far-off standards unprintable, was enough to commend a thing to Henry Hammond's notebook. Home from the Crumms, pencil in hand, he pressed the pages open.

He recorded his latest inspiration.

Next he wrote: 'Elephants! Whales? Sperm Whales!?'

As usual he was polishing a jewel against the day when some story or poem would shine more original because of it. But this time, after the sperm whales, he stopped. He laid his chin in the heel of his hand. He was thinking about love and sex in terms of that tiny bubble of spit and the unity of his imagination. Unity in diversity. There was the knights and vigils side too. It was all very encouraging. He wondered how soon it would be possible to make a definite forward move.

The cost and use of objects had a new interest for him. He wanted to touch furniture. He read advertisements of gas cookers, dustbins, anything, even toothpaste for two had to be reckoned, he trod differently on carpets now, and he knew about mortgages. At the end of half an hour with a Chelsea estate agent he told the man, 'We won't be getting married yet,' and his throat clenched over the words. He felt his emotion scald him with the keenest interest, it was so promising. He visited some addresses the agent had given. They were fashionably expensive, all of them, and he warned himself (he was often facetious with himself), Don't be previous, while he admired views and quartered urban gardens and struggled to sort out domesticity's kinds.

Loud enough for the paper-knife to hear, but only just, Henry Hammond murmured, 'Beyond a peradventure.' There was no question where it pointed. It pointed at the telephone.

So he picked the knife up and reconsidered.

He fondled it.

He could not carry her off on a wave of small distinguished *objets*. That, he thought, was precisely the problem. He must think. His plan of life was based on a discipline and a decorum which, from good shoes upwards, must be examined again very thoroughly. These first years were all-important. During them the new writer would emerge and be identified with the already known young publisher. That was the plan, and it did not so much require changing as enlarging, Henry Hammond now told himself. But he needed time to think and organise. (It never occurred to him she might like him more or less as he was.) He had actually avoided her this last fortnight, choosing unlikely times for coming and going, always on guard at corners. He kept clear of her probable route between office and Long Acre. Once he thought he saw her in Henrietta Street and bolted into the nearest shop. It was raining and the side of her face (if it was she) was wet. She was looking the other way.

In any case, a fortnight spent like this had its compensations. Speaking of 'my fiancée' was a great joy the afternoon he did his house-hunting—so great that he feared all possible outcomes. The daytime wives in houses for sale prolonged it—the joy—with questions about her. He would always remember one of them by her special knowing modesty and sweetness. She was completely at ease in the bedrooms, and he liked whatever it was he shared with her when kitchen layout happened to be their theme and he had to confess ignorance of his future wife's opinions. They stood side by side laughing and looking across each other. She showed him her jars of bottled fruit. Row on row. They looked odd in a smart town house, he thought.

At the Crumms it was possible to speak Anne Trematon's name and to be practical. Gedge needed discussing. It made solid sense to get involved in her affairs, really her brother's affairs, but that will make no difference (so Henry Hammond reasoned) when it is discovered that I have been quietly doing good. Doing good will help, not as much as arriving, but it will help. Some of my ambitions might be paltry, if I were less remarkable.

He returned to the bubble of spit, and then he decided. He lifted an envelope and a sheet of paper from the drawer of his desk. He wrote: *Dear Anne.* It shone. But the room was now nearly dark, so he got up and turned the light on. Back in his chair he found *Dear Anne* different but no less wonderful. Love in books did not begin.

> *Dear Anne,*
> *Can a whole fortnight*

He frowned into the future. In books written up to now, he qualified. He tore up the sheet of paper and found another.

> *Dear Anne,*
> *Bless me! Can a whole fortnight have passed since I had supper with you? That evening remains, for me, an island of peace in an ocean of noise and bustle. Time is standing on its head these days. I seem to be perpetually awing—literally awing. The truth is, I have just flown back overnight from the South American Book Fair in Rio—you may have seen the fuss in the papers—and before I become engulfed again I want*

He stopped and read over. A prudent emotion was awakened by *The truth is.* He tore up what he had written.

> *Anne,*
> *Bless me dear Anne! A whole fortnight has passed and*

So far so good, Henry Hammond judged.

15

THE Post Office van was being driven at great speed, as if to disappear down St. John's Wood High Street.

However it stopped beside a pillar box.

By the time David arrived its driver was scooping the mail into his sack. He was head and shoulders inside the box, and a bunch of keys dangled from the open door.

David waited. He coughed.

'Drop it in then,' the postman said, not looking up.

David answered, 'I'm trying to find Melbourne Court; it's somewhere in this postal district.'

'No such place—not in St. John's Wood.'

The postman withdrew his head from the body of the box, and asked, 'You don't mean Melbourne *House*, by any chance?'

'That might be it.'

'Melbourne *House*?'

'Perhaps I do.'

'You do you know.'

I hope I do, he thought, when the way the postman sent him led along narrow side roads, to the narrowest of all, almost an alley. Garbage on the pavement. This was what he wanted. He counted three greengrocers.

A gap appeared on his left, a square of land, bombed, with new brick buildings facing inwards on the other three sides. In the middle of the fourth side, David's side, was a notice planted in a round of grass the size of a large cartwheel. A sort of tin ticket stuck in the grass said *Keep Off the Grass*, and the notice itself said:

ADELAIDE HOUSE

MELBOURNE HOUSE   SYDNEY HOUSE

LONDON COUNTY COUNCIL

So he turned towards the left-hand building along a path of concrete blocks.

Inside it reminded him of an army drill-hall where the quartet had shared a concert once, on a dark afternoon, with a semi-professional choir from Nuneaton. The walls were brown to waist height, and after that a weak pink on and on to the ceiling. A football had been kicked or thrown against the wall, as the print of leather segments showed. He saw a door with CARETAKER'S FLAT on it and bars of light shining through the ribbed glass. An old man answered the bell.

David said, 'I'm sorry to trouble you.'

The man answered, 'Oh yes.'

David gave him time to add something else, and then said, 'I am looking for a Mr. Hammond.' The man still said nothing so David went on, 'He did say his address was Melbourne Court, but I think he must have meant Melbourne House.'

'Some of them do say Melbourne Court,' said the old man at last, breaking into a most serene smile, 'then again some of them say Melbourne Place, and I've heard Melbourne Grange, and Villas. And when there was a fire in Sixteen I carried out an armful of writing paper stamped Melbourne Mansions. Stamped Mansions (I'm telling you, boy) stamped, not written, on every page. And I'll tell you something else. When I was caretaker at the John Burns Building down in Stepney, the Africans there used to say John Burns Paradise, some of them. They wrote Paradise too, those as could write, not meaning to deceive because they put Buildings underneath in case the Post Office wouldn't know. They weren't ashamed of being L.C.C., not like a lot of these here.'

At random, his mind racing off, David asked chasing blood, 'Why did they call it Paradise, the Africans?'

'They called it Paradise because it was Paradise,' the old man replied, and directed him to Nineteen.

David began to climb the stairs.

He was thinking, I was right. There *was* something funny about where he lived.

Today was Friday. On Tuesday night, though not very late, Anne returned to Long Acre with a strange and powerful smell on her breath which she said was garlic. She had been eating in Soho with Henry Hammond who had written a letter inviting her. David studied her closely for other signs apart from the garlic, but could find none except that at breakfast next morning she mentioned a plan the two of them had made. Before long, in the next week or two, Henry Hammond proposed to look in after supper with some gramophone records. David watched her intently. 'Here?' he said. She replied, 'It's no trouble. Henry says these new long-playing records weigh nothing at all.' 'But our gramophone won't play long-playing records.' 'I know. I told him. He is bringing his gramophone as well. He said it would be more fun here.' David just looked at her. He was thinking *More fun!*—and then he suddenly remembered Dr. Hennessy's words about Henry Hammond being a pretender, and yesterday, Thursday, he phoned Smith and Nordenfeld from the Academy and asked for his address. That was interesting. The girl at the switchboard said she kept all home addresses, but when she looked she found his was missing and had to go away and get it from the staff file.

Still climbing the stairs, David began to patch up a reason for coming. So far he had been too busy following the trail to worry. I'll say I was passing and dropped in, he had thought in so far as he did think. He must improve on that. But he still did not worry. Dr. Hennessy's medicine, which he was taking as directed, placed an invisible film between him and worrying. All the movements of his body felt very slightly late. This was not affecting his music as far as he could tell, but he did not worry about that either. Realising that he was not worrying in the old way was the nearest he got to worrying. He was sleeping well. The medicine was turning their kitchen spoon a rusty green.

I'll find a better reason for coming, he told himself in his new peaceful postponing mood, listening to a baby which had started to cry somewhere in the building, merely heeding it, letting the bodiless spurts of sound lap round him, like what? like rending calico he decided with lazy satisfaction.

Stone steps. Iron banister rail. On the pink wall a pencilled fledged arrow transfixed a flat heart.

The nastier the better, David thought, to make him even more ashamed of being L.C.C., until he leaves her alone and goes away. I don't care where he goes.

These were fierce thoughts but he formed them almost drowsily.

He wanted to stretch, like too much sun.

It had occurred to him to wonder if his medicine was the same only smaller doses as the handy stuff Dr. Hennessy said he was giving Mr. Gedge.

Between the baby's cries he heard somebody cross the hall below and start climbing. The man—he could tell it was a man coming up behind him—decided him to leave now. David saw that his mission was accomplished. He would leave quietly and work out how to use what he knew. He did not need a reason for coming.

He stood at the top of the stairs waiting to go down. No doubt he appeared to be hesitating, because the man asked him cheerily, 'Are you lost?' David said, 'No' and the man replied, 'Well I am. Where would I find Nineteen?' 'That's where I was going,' said David with a dreamy imprudence also brought on by his medicine. The man suggested they went together. He carried a stick, and once he was walking on the flat had an evident limp. He showed no interest in the nature of David's visit, but surveyed their gloomy surroundings as they went, and remarked in the same jovial way, 'There's safety in numbers.'

Outside the door of Nineteen, breathing heavily, the man pressed the bell and with a quick turn to David asked, 'Do you know this one?

> 'Off to hounds one fine day with the Quorn
> I grew an unquenchable horn.
> "Good God!" cried a huntsman,
> "We aren't after those, man!
> It's foxes not fuxes this morn."'

He gave David a Thumbs Up sign while the door was being opened in their faces.

16

MRS. HAMMOND cut across the conversation and said, 'Cheer up, son! It can't hardly be as bad as that.'

The others regarded David with mild interest before resuming their talk, while he composed his expression differently.

He was surprised. From the inside his face had already seemed, before she spoke, to be wearing of its own accord a fixed, rather stupid happy look which belonged to the well-fed sensation of these days of purple medicine. Perhaps I look in every way unlike what I feel, he conjectured without distress, philosophically. To Mrs. Hammond he said, 'I'm enjoying myself'—and then, in easy disconnection, 'I really came to see your other son, Henry.'

'Harry,' she said, and shook her head slowly to indicate the size of the subject.

Earlier, when her husband opened the door of Nineteen to David and the limping man, Mr. Clive Turgoose, he showed them to the living-room and announced the occasion: 'Gentlemen of the press to interview Samuel as per appointment.' All of them there, Mr. and Mrs. Hammond, Sammy, Sammy's sister, and the neighbour who called for a minute, ignored David. At first they took him for some kind of assistant to Mr. Turgoose like a runner or a caddie. But when they heard there was going to be at least one picture in next week's paper, they assumed he was the photographer.

Mr. Turgoose's method was to say he was a rugger man himself, so Sammy would have to explain everything very simply. Then he sat with his notebook open, and Sammy talked. His family, mainly his sister, kept interrupting. She remembered more than he could about the boys who had played with him for Ordnance Road Juniors, and what they were doing now. 'Attagirl!' said Mr. Turgoose, 'this is just what our readers want to hear about. The further away someone goes, like the one—I've got his name—who is fighting Communists in Malaya today, the more interested they are. It doesn't matter if they know him personally.' He consulted his shorthand notes and asked Sammy to proceed. His baggy tweed suit and stick made him look more like a farmer, David thought, than a London reporter.

After Ordnance Road Juniors came Camden Town Boys, then London Schoolboys, then a trial for the England Youth team (he didn't quite make that one) and finally Charlton Athletic.

'I have my first game—for the Reserves mind—next Saturday,' Sammy said. His manner was sullen and had been so throughout. This proved to be his version of modesty. Every few seconds he shot a glance at his mother whose eyes were bent down upon her sewing. He was obviously Henry Hammond's brother, they both had the same coarse black hair, tending to curl. David reckoned they could be Spaniards, the boys—not the parents, nor the sister who was fair and had a round face and tiny nose. David liked her. From the way she looked at Mr. Turgoose's notebook, she either knew shorthand or was very curious.

There was a parrot in the corner which kept saying, 'I'm Billy Mitchell.' Afterwards Mr. Turgoose told David he wished he had had the teaching of it. His eyes were moist at the thought. Another skill the parrot possessed was to make its cage shudder and swing without itself appearing to move.

Mrs. Hammond was stitching buttons. She said nothing. Mr. Hammond interposed 'True' now and then, sometimes 'True, true,' but otherwise he too was silent, until Mr. Turgoose remarked to Sammy in a summarising tone, 'And so you are now a fully-fledged professional footballer.' 'From today when I signed my forms like,' Sammy answered;

130

at which his father broke in, 'Your *contract*, Samuel,' and Sammy registered something like dismay.

For the first and only time, in the pause which followed, the parrot said, 'Have a cigar.'

Mr. Hammond reproached it absently, and then talked about the law. It appeared that Charlton Athletic Football Club had drafted a document which 'you could drive a coach and four through.' The phrase impressed David. He had never heard it before. He heard it again nearly twenty years later, from the doctor who examined his wife before her first baby. He disliked it then and suspected all doctors, but as Mr. Hammond used it there was no question of the Club being unfair to Sammy. On the contrary, one of the clauses was framed so loosely, according to Mr. Hammond, that Sammy could have taken advantage of his employer if he had been a rogue. 'Look at it like this. The playing season is nearly finished. Samuel has a game or two, he draws his wage through the summer for doing next to nothing, and when full-time training starts again he repudiates his contract. What can the other party do about that?'

'Sue him,' said Mr. Turgoose a trifle impatiently.

'Sue a minor? You know Sam's age.'

'Come now, squire! This is 1947!'

Mr. Turgoose's arm effected a sweeping, billowing motion, to dismiss technicalities, and perhaps to suggest the rising moral standard of the world.

'Does that mean,' asked David, responding to a mental zest which touched him quite often in those days, 'that the contract is illegal?'

Sammy and Dawn met each other's eye. Mrs. Hammond plied her needle as before. But Mr. Hammond stretched out his legs, and, smiling blissfully at his shoes, said, 'Not *illegal*. The contract is legal—*lawful* we say—but it is not legally *enforceable*.'

'I'm Billy Mitchell,' said the parrot, a split second ahead of Mr. Turgoose who said, 'Fancy.'

'Lawful but not enforceable at law.'

Having repeated this distinction in its naked force and majesty, Mr. Hammond turned and addressed himself to David alone, half asserting, half questioning, 'You understand what I'm saying.'

Flustered by Mr. Hammond's ardour, David replied, 'I'm not sure.'

Sammy and Dawn looked at each other again in heavy anticipation, but this time Mr. Turgoose was ready. He said to Sammy, 'We must have a picture of you signing that contract;' and when Sammy reiterated that it had been signed already, this morning in the Manager's office, Mr. Turgoose told him 'Not to worry,' newspapers didn't work like that, all that was needed was a table and chair, a piece of paper and a pen—'and you' he added in his humorous style. He surveyed the room and said he must leave arrangements to his colleague. 'Pictures! Let's have some pictures!' He pretended to spit on his hands. 'On with the show!'

It was now that the others discovered David was not the photographer. 'You are very welcome I'm sure,' said Dawn, but nobody asked him why he was there, and somehow a good moment to explain never arrived.

Mr. Turgoose left the room and was heard shouting from a passage window down into the area below.

'Old Winny is always on the dot,' he said when he returned.

'Guess how old she is,' Mrs. Hammond demanded sharply. She meant the parrot. She continued at once, 'Thirty-two. Aren't you, Billy? Aren't you, eh? Who's my little bugger? You're an old man, you're past it, Billy. Aren't you then?' Mr. Turgoose surveyed the silent bird and exclaimed 'Wotcher!' in non-committal greeting. 'Mother is that fond of him,' said Dawn.

The door-bell rang. Mr. Hammond answered it and returned with the *Marylebone Telegraph* photographer, a Mr. Winn, who politely hoped the talking was over and he wasn't too early; and on the other hand he hoped he wasn't too late, he had been delayed at Swiss Cottage where a prize-winning stall was most unattractively arranged when he got there. 'Winny takes his art seriously,' said Mr. Turgoose. 'I do,' Mr. Winn replied, and went on telling them and sorting out his equipment. He talked while he worked. The treasures of the Swiss Cottage Women's Institute had burnt an ear against her oven door. She had been listening to a cake. He thought she looked becoming in a head-bandage, but they could judge for themselves in next week's *Telegraph*. Did they know, he asked, that the greatest experts decided when a cake was cooked by the sound it made?

Mrs. Hammond did not believe him. She was frank about it.

Mr. Hammond said you should keep an open mind.

Mr. Winn took several photographs of Sammy, head and shoulders, by flashlight although it was early evening and still bright sun outside. Then he lent him a heavy old fountain pen and posed him for signing his contract.

'Is that the lot?' asked Sammy.

'I should like a family group,' said Mr. Winn. 'It could be most agreeable.'

'Harry's not here,' said Dawn.

'We will do without him,' stated Mr. Hammond as a fact, and they clustered together. When Mrs. Hammond got up to join her husband and children, David noticed she was wearing bedroom slippers. He and Mr. Turgoose stood behind Mr. Winn, who rearranged the others, explaining 'I want you to look natural.' Mr. Turgoose suggested that they should include the parrot in their group.

Mr. Winn ignored Mr. Turgoose and took his photograph. He appeared grave, even dissatisfied, when he had finished. 'I'm Billy Mitchell,' said the parrot. 'Yes,' said Mr. Winn thoughtfully, and then he asked Sammy if by any chance there was a football in the flat. Because, he said, a study of him holding a football could be felicitous. 'In keeping,' he added.

But there was no football in the flat.

Mr. Turgoose said, 'What a pity' and asked Mr. Winn for a lift home. 'I saw the van outside,' said Mr. Turgoose. 'I don't mind the old van, I'd rather shake than walk any day.'

'Trevor Pringle has a football,' said Dawn.

Sammy blushed and agreed that this was true.

They all hesitated until Sammy led the way out, saying Trevor Pringle was only a little kid. Both parents stayed behind. David also waited because he had an urge to say thank you, he wasn't sure for what.

'This is Harry's room,' said Mrs. Hammond immediately. She showed him an ordinary small bedroom except there was a table, and books stacked on the floor. David didn't know what to say. She could see he didn't. She opened the wardrobe and said, 'There's his dinner-suit.' Then she said, 'He's at the office, he works that hard.'

Mrs. Hammond said, 'You will be a bit younger than him.'

They were back in the living-room.

Mr Hammond said, 'I expect you are pals.'

'We have a friend in common,' said David.

They said nothing. They were regarding him earnestly and warmly but not inquisitively. They wanted nothing out of him. Nevertheless he told them about Mr. Gedge. He knew it might bring trouble. It was certainly unnecessary. The result was impossible to guess, let alone control. He just did it. It was true he felt middle-class talking about a friend in common, but this was not a reason. He was not ashamed of hating Henry Hammond and he liked the parents all the more for being proud of, almost for being the parents of Henry Hammond, and this was absolutely mysterious to him in a carefree way.

But for the purple medicine he might have left at once. As it was, he stayed and told them about Mr. Gedge.

When he had finished, Mrs. Hammond said 'Poor gentleman,' and asked how Mr. Gedge was now. Of course David could not tell her. He must have seemed neglectful but there it was, he did not propose to talk about Henry Hammond and Anne and his patch of bad sleeping. He let them think he had been busy with his music and no time for anything else. Then an idea occurred to him. He had not thought of it before. He said, 'The clergyman—the Reverend Crumm. I told you Mr. Gedge interrupted his sermon and spent the night in his house before going to Hyde Park. The clergyman promised me he would make sure they were looking after him properly in hospital.' The Reverend Crumm had not said this. The idea felt true, however.

'A clergyman is best for those things,' said Mrs. Hammond.

'I'm Billy Mitchell,' said the parrot.

'My maiden name, see? I was a Mitchell.'

Mr. Hammond gathered the other two human beings within his gaze and said, 'I have been thinking. You may agree or you may not. But in my respectful submission, on the evidence so far deposed the aforesaid gentleman has been unlawfully distrained. I know what you will say—'

He raised an arm.

'Like father like son,' Mrs. Hammond whispered. 'You should hear him and Harry together.'

'—it will be objected that Mr. Gedge's presence in hospital implies a willingness to establish contractual relations. In my submission, no such construction can be placed upon the facts, and from the young gentleman's testimony the hospital authorities may be indicted with Malfeasance to wit False Pretences and further to which Wrongful Detention, and on behalf of the plaintiff's wife (if any) a common law writ will lie in respect to Enticement of Spouse.'

'He has no wife.'

Mr. Hammond looked at David blankly.

'And if we make a fuss, won't they certify him, and then he can't come out of hospital at all?'

Mr. Hammond rose in answer and removed a book called *Be Your Own Lawyer*, one of five or six, from a wall-bracket above his head.

He stood fumbling with it. The room seemed airless now, and smaller. Far away a noise could be heard.

'That clergyman must watch out,' Mrs. Hammond said, 'in case they do experiments on your Mr. Gedge. We don't know, is he on the panel? The panel's not like private. They get experimental on panel patients. Or they might want to make an exhibit of him in front of their students.'

'Listen!' said Mr. Hammond.

'I'm Billy Mitchell,' said the parrot.

Mrs. Hammond was listening already. She too could hear the distant noise. 'Daddy,' said she softly to her husband, and she inclined an ear towards the outside world, 'what is it if it isn't skylarking again?'

He opened his mouth, evidently to hear better.

'That's what it is,' he confirmed.

'Then,' she said, 'talking's no good at all. You must create.'

He moved to go. It was clear he hoped she would stay behind, he tried to take leave of her and David, but Mrs. Hammond said she was coming on after, and David found himself hurriedly following Mr. Hammond out of the room.

The knocking noise came from the hall of the building, mixed with shouting and laughing. It rose up the staircase to meet them. David thought he distinguished Dawn's voice, but as the bend of steps unfurled beneath his feet and revealed the scene below, he saw it was a small boy. Across the hall had been placed a line of red fire buckets filled with sand, a few feet apart. The boy stood at one end of the line. A football lay at his feet. Sammy stood at the other end with a stopwatch. 'Go!' he shouted. The boy ran in and out of the fire buckets kicking the ball along with him; at the last bucket he turned and doubled back weaving as before, in and out, and stopped where he had started. 'Thirteen and seven-tenths,' called Sammy, 'that's nearly half a second faster than last time.' At which the boy—he was quite small—gave a scream and ran to Sammy and looked up into his face. Sammy responded by catching him by his jacket lapels and shaking him pleasantly, while Mr. Turgoose emerged from the shadows, and bent down and for some reason squinted along the line of buckets.

Mr. Hammond cried 'Samuel!' with urgent force, from the bottom of the staircase. 'Samuel! You know what Ma said.'

David could hear the slip-slop of bedroom slippers behind him. Mrs. Hammond was still invisible.

'Don't you burst your braces, Dad,' said Sammy. 'We were just showing these gentlemen Trevor's routine. There's nothing beats the buckets for ball-control. It's a workout, see. It's training.' He winked at his father over the small boy's head. His sulkiness had vanished. And then without warning, as it were insanely, he shouted 'Up the Dynamoes!' and snatched the football and dropped it at his own feet and set off at top speed among the buckets.

When he raised his head again his mother was in view.

After a bit of searching he found the words 'This is special, Ma.' She made no answer, and he went on 'And Dawn's here this time.'

Dawn stepped forward and said 'Mr. Adams says it is all right.'

David recognised the caretaker who now retired behind the ribbed glass of his front door.

'Who moved the buckets?'

Sammy made to speak. Mrs. Hammond told him, 'Then you put them back.'

The photographer, Mr. Winn, admitted in a resolute voice that he had helped to move the buckets. Mrs. Hammond glared at him and asked if he had finished taking his pictures. He answered rather haughtily, 'In a sense. But of course my work is never done.'

She grunted.

Dawn began, 'Mr. Adams says—'

'And what will Mr. Adams say when the Council agent comes again about the complaints? He'll say the same as last time.' Mrs. Hammond turned full on her daughter.

'He'll say "Some of them do make a lot of noise".'

'That was nothing to do with us,' said Dawn boldly, 'it was the singing when the pubs shut.'

But Mr. Turgoose already had a bucket in each hand. So had Mr. Winn. David grabbed two more for himself. One had to be quick. Sammy was on his second journey.

Heavy stuff, sand.

'Where does this go?' David said, half to himself.

An educated voice replied 'Anywhere. Just get rid of it.'

Henry Hammond was standing at his elbow.

17

EACH recognised the other snap together.

'I didn't see it was you,' said Henry Hammond.

'It's you,' said David.

A big effort climbed into Henry Hammond's eyes. A neck muscle stirred and he said lightly, 'My mother seems to be on the rampage.'

'Yes,' David said, as slow as possible, telling himself to behave unreassuringly, his first surprise turning towards a cruel yet sleepy expectation. He thought (in these very words) Let him château d'yquem his way out of this one. If he can.

If he can.

I hate him.

I hate him.

They faced each other.

'Many hands make light work,' said Henry Hammond, seizing a bucket. 'Though at the same time, too many cooks spoil the broth. Have you noticed, David, how those old saws run in contradictory pairs?'

Thinking, I'll make him pay, David returned a level impudent childish stare. On and on.

'Out of sight out of mind,' said Henry Hammond a bit faster, 'but distance lends enchantment to the view.'

He'll leave us alone (David thought) when I have finished with him.

David called to Mr. Winn, 'The whole family is here now for your photograph.'

'Ah,' said Mr. Winn.

'No time like the present,' said Mr. Turgoose.

Sammy punched his brother facetiously in greeting and tried to ruffle his hair. Dawn kissed him. She said he looked tired.

Henry Hammond said nothing.

Mr. Winn asked them all to come outside, and to bring the football which would be more in keeping outside. It could be a very pleasing study. 'Only when everything's tidy in here,' Mrs. Hammond said. They stayed until it was.

Then Henry Hammond led the way with his crisp stride and glamour. He wants to get it over, David thought. Mrs. Hammond came last. Her two younger children were teasing her about something.

The Hammond family formed up.

Mr. Winn used a tripod this time. He was fixing his camera on it when Mr. Hammond said, 'One moment!'— David thought he was going to make a legal remark—and then, 'What do folks think?' Nobody took much notice of him. Sammy told Dawn to show a leg, which amused Mr. Turgoose but not Mr. Winn. Mr. Winn was humming 'Drinking Rum and Coca-Cola'. He was busy fixing and focussing.

'One moment!' said Mr. Hammond again, looking round happily as though he liked being ignored. 'Let's make it a real get-together.'

'Tell us, squire,' said Mr. Turgoose who was not really attending any more than the others.

Mr. Hammond explained, 'Let's all get this side of the camera, friends as well as family.'

As it happened Henry Hammond was standing next to his father, looking tired as Dawn had said, anyhow he looked odd, and Mr. Hammond said to him, 'Won't your pal join us?'

Mrs. Hammond added, 'You haven't introduced your friend, Harry.'

While David and Henry Hammond eyed one another little Trevor Pringle ran forward and asked 'Can I be in the picture?'

'But surely!' said Henry Hammond. 'And I hope David will too.'

'You're the team mascot like,' Sammy told the small boy, and propelled him to the front.

'This is my friend David'—like that, with no surname; and David allowed Henry Hammond's black eyes to spend themselves on him, before answering 'It would be a pity to spoil the family group. No, I think I will watch from over here for a minute, and then slip away.'

But he stayed to the end, which was very soon, and then the Hammond family retired into Melbourne House, and Mr. Turgoose and Mr. Winn prepared to drive off.

'Can we give you a lift?' Mr. Winn invited him. 'At least I hope we can.' He fished in the pocket of his corduroy jacket and produced an ignition key. 'Ah yes,' he said in his gentlest tone. 'Excellent!'

'Easy as kiss my arse,' said Mr. Turgoose, as David hesitated in front of the pre-war *Marylebone Telegraph* van and its two seats; and he threw open the back doors to reveal a squat little chair on the floor of the van, amid photographic and other equipment. 'Veronica carries three sitting,' Mr. Turgoose said, 'but standing—' He paused. 'She prefers an erection of passengers. Don't you, you old nymphomaniac?' And he rapped her battered side with his stick. 'We all share her in the office,' he said, and David climbed in and sat facing backwards.

Then something happened which he was expecting in his drowsy malice all mixed up with the purple medicine, at least it fitted his mood. Mr. Winn was stowing his tripod and Mr. Turgoose was limping around looking too hot in his tweeds. The back doors of the van were open. David was actually thinking how he would not like to kiss Mr. Turgoose's arse, when, through the doors of the van, he saw Henry Hammond run out of Melbourne House and stop and look about him. He saw David, and came and stood outside the van. David sat throned inside.

'David,' he said, 'we didn't really have time to say hullo.'

'It was rather a crowd.' David waved in the direction of

141

Melbourne House. 'Quite a crowd,' he said.

Henry Hammond laughed. Then, 'And how's Anne?'

'She's very well. She's fine, thank you. She will be waiting to hear about my day, specially this part of it.'

Henry Hammond laughed again.

'I wouldn't make too much of it,' he said.

He laughed again.

'I hope you won't, David.'

This time David laughed. 'Look!' he said. 'There's the shorthand notebook. On the seat in front. It's funny to think it tells everything that happened.'

'Well then,' said Henry Hammond, withdrawing a pace and bending stiffly from the waist in his Schnabel bow, 'please remember me to Anne.'

Mr. Winn shut the van doors and climbed in. Mr. Turgoose was in already.

'Home, James!' said Mr. Turgoose.

But they did not move. Mr. Winn was struggling with some object out of sight. He pushed and pulled, then rested, then pushed and pulled again, then placed his hands over the steering wheel and laid his head sideways on top of them. 'This is always happening,' he said. David thought the engine had broken down. Next, however, with no trouble, Mr. Winn started the engine. It sounded normal. But the van began to move backwards. 'I thought so,' said Mr. Winn quietly, and they stopped and he got out. At that moment Henry Hammond opened the back doors and asked, 'Is anything wrong?'

Mr. Winn explained that a thing called the gear selector had jammed in reverse, so the van would only go backwards.

'You know what the Duke of Wellington used to say on these occasions?' said Mr. Turgoose.

'I have no doubt,' replied Mr. Winn, suddenly flushing, 'that I should find it disagreeable, Turgoose.' In his ordinary voice he continued, 'The gearbox cover must come off; I shan't keep you more than five minutes.'

'A minor operation!' said Henry Hammond. 'Then you and I have just got time to stroll to the end of the road and back. Haven't we, David?'

He can wait for his answer (David thought) while Mr. Winn folded his soft green jacket over the seat and rolled up his sleeves. A neat man. By his side stood Mr. Turgoose, who scarcely spoke again. There were midges in the air almost like summer.

Climbing down to the ground, David said, 'I'd rather stay here and watch. I don't know a thing about engines.'

The van's floormat, more holes than mat, lay on the concrete where Mr. Winn had thrown it out. He held a screwdriver. Henry Hammond joined David and the two men, and he bent his head.

'David,' he said.

Mr. Winn then asked the others for a little more elbow room. They stood back, and he began removing the lid of an iron lump in the floor of the van.

'It's a business of too many cooks again,' said Henry Hammond.

David pretended not to understand.

'We aren't wanted,' Henry Hammond said. 'Do take a stroll with me.'

David said, 'Look!'

The lid was off.

He pointed at the metal nest of cogs and rods, and exclaimed to Mr. Winn who was dabbling in thick wispy grease, 'Poor you! It must be complicated.'

Mr. Winn glanced up as if his ear had heard something false. 'I shan't keep you much longer,' he said. And at that moment Henry Hammond cleared his throat and proclaimed generally, 'I have something to discuss with David. If you two gentlemen will excuse us—'

'Some other time, perhaps,' David murmured. He saw no end to this pleasure, and its variations. But Mr. Winn issued what was nothing less than a command. 'Go this minute,' he said, 'don't hurry, and I will treat myself to a wash when I have finished.' He showed them the clots of grease on his well-kept hands.

Turning away alongside Henry Hammond, David swore he would pay for this as well.

'That brother of mine, he's a characterful young man.'

He tried again, 'I always call him The Card.'

And again, 'He calls me The City Slicker.'

And again, 'We get on surprisingly well.'

And again, 'I'm glad you witnessed the football interview. Humble stuff, of course. Very local news. Things were hectic at the office or I should have been with you contributing my mite.'

'Do you mean,' said David, 'you are interested in football too? I thought it was odd at the time, when you told us about the club named after the runner which had nothing to do with sport.'

'The Pheidippides is a dining club.'

'So you said.'

'I'm not a liar.'

Silence is the best answer, David reckoned.

'What are you doing here?'

'I came to see you about Mr. Gedge.'

'Has something happened?'

'Not so far as I know. I just wanted to talk to you.'

'Good,' said Henry Hammond. 'And now you are here, let me say how much I hope we shall be friends. You see, I have fallen in love with your sister. With Anne,' he added.

'She is very beautiful.'

'I know,' said Henry Hammond humbly and yet thrusting on, 'I know. In a few months I will have my own place. I'm only perching here. A flat. I'm thinking of Chelsea. Perhaps a small house.'

'Why?'

Henry Hammond glanced sideways and took stock of David. 'Well,' he said, 'I expect she has lots of friends. Admirers. About Anne and myself, I'm not assuming—

Chelsea or anywhere—she may never care to join forces with me.'

It sounded old-fashioned even then to talk about joining forces. David guessed that his enemy did not dare to be more outspoken. Perhaps he felt doomed already.

David basked in this possibility. Finally he said, 'Yes, Anne has many friends.'

Then he recalled the dinner in Soho, the garlic.

The waiting for her.

'We are both very busy. We do almost everything together.'

'I know you are close,' said Henry Hammond gravely.

And then Henry Hammond said, 'That's why I want us— you and me—to be friends, David. I don't just mean because of Anne. Love doesn't work like that. I mean really you and me. Really friends. We have so much to give each other. Your music for example; I adore music. Though I am ignorant,' he declared in his new-found modesty. He uttered a conscious little laugh. 'You must teach me.'

'What have you got to give me?' David asked. Henry Hammond's words had uncovered yet another way of hurting him, but in doing this they changed everything else. They were fateful. While the answer to them came, 'Surely that's not for me to say,' David's sensation of command, easy, indolent, complete, went solid into bricks and mortar. He saw exactly what to do.

He felt invulnerable.

He said, 'Then *I* will say.'

Henry Hammond had stopped too. They were standing in the middle of the road, a quiet empty road.

'You can help me with Mr. Gedge. Like this. When I asked you at supper with us, could you get his book published, you said, "I think I could force it through my board but it would make me a laughing stock in the trade." I'm not making this up, I wouldn't know the expressions, I'm remembering what you said.'

'That's right,' said Henry Hammond.

'Well?'

'Actually your question was could I get it taken *if I wanted to.*'

If I say 'well?' again, or if I just look at him, he will say he doesn't want to, David thought, and I prefer to hurt him somewhere else first. He said, 'Let's stick to the point which is what can you give me. You think you *could* get his book published.'

'One throws off all sorts of remarks at the dinner table.'

'Supper table.'

'Supper table. I may have exaggerated my influence.'

'But you can still do your best.'

'As I say, I may have misled you. We all talk recklessly sometimes.'

'A pity,' said David. He looked up into the ugly face of Melbourne House. 'Anne will be disappointed too. Anyhow you can do your best.'

'My best really isn't worth doing over this matter.'

'I suppose,' said David, speaking very slowly, 'the amount of influence someone has in his work depends a bit on his home background. And everything else about him. I mean everything is affected by the sort of family he comes from.'

Henry Hammond said nothing.

'I wondered why you ran out of the front door or entrance, whatever it's called, and asked me not to make too much of my visit here to Anne.'

'David,' answered Henry Hammond then, 'you have an extraordinarily clear memory for the things I say. You will also remember that I believe Gedge's book to be meritless. I told you so plainly. Neither you nor Anne would expect me to press the claim of a work I had no faith in.'

'You said it was only fit for lavatory paper.'

'I should like to apologise for suggesting that.'

'I don't want you to apologise.'

'Why not, David?'

'I hate you. I will always hate you. Leave us alone. Go away and stay away.'

146

18

BUT for that outburst David would never have kept his appointment with Dr. Hennessy. Gradually, over the last few days, he had decided not to turn up. No explanations. No letter. He was well, and being well he would disappear from the medical scene and get on with life; and he told himself Dr. Hennessy would approve, at least secretly.

Now, or rather in bed that night, after Melbourne House, he changed his mind. His appointment was the next afternoon. He lay in bed and decided to go. He was thinking about 'I hate you' which certainly called for thought because it had taken him by surprise. There was no question and no fear of being ill again, but a sort of inside gap had appeared. David tried to be precise. This evening, walking with Henry Hammond, he was in complete control and messed it up. What I was and what I did must be different, he reasoned, at least they were different then. I messed it up because I messed it up, not because I could not help it. I could help it.

He did the meeting with Henry Hammond over again in bed, this time not messing it up. Instead of 'I hate you' David tormented him along the whole length of the road they had taken earlier but followed only so far. Inevitably, this evening, 'I hate you' had brought the end. They were both so shocked by it. Henry Hammond muttered something about having wanted to be friends, and then he remembered where he was, declaring 'So it's going to be a fight, David, this is nature red in tooth and claw,' and David echoed 'Tooth and claw,' also in a daze, near disbelief, and there they had parted.

In bed, David kept them on the same road, on and on,

expertly. He held and squeezed the idea that they had a lot to give each other. Telling Henry Hammond he could help Mr. Gedge, that was what he could give, was only the beginning. Modest help was better than no help. The thing to be honest about was how modest, and David wrung every drop from that vainglorious picture of the job with Smith and Nordenfeld. Then he turned to Melbourne Court and Melbourne House. He made Henry Hammond bend in shame under the most full, distinct correction. He made him confess that he had been striving to appear acceptable to Anne, and now he must despair.

'Not entirely,' David answered (still in bed of course), eyeing him, making him wait and suffer.

Henry Hammond did not dare ask what he meant, so David told him: he could nevertheless do his little best for Mr. Gedge and thus hope to win credit. 'Your best might not be worthless,' David admonished him from a very great height: which was Henry Hammond's cue to plead that Anne would only despise him the more for his insincerity. 'You are back in your old groove,' said David, seeing and commanding all, 'you can't believe in Mr. Gedge's book. You don't understand how important it is. Well you must.'

Henry Hammond undertook to be diligent.

'Then listen,' David said.

He talked. He had not read the whole book by any means. He explained this sternly and frankly, but saying he knew Mr. Gedge and that was enough, he could do the rest by himself. And so he talked, and Henry Hammond stood as before a jealous god.

This part, as he lay in the dark and imagined it, took ages. It enfolded both the wisdom and the cunning of David's purpose, which 'I hate you' had wantonly thrown away. Love itself, and truth, were served in his praise of Mr. Gedge, and by the same token Henry Hammond was tricked into an endless painful wait, in suit of Anne. What's more, he might succeed in getting the book published, he was desperate, it was not impossible. However grossly he had exaggerated his influence with Smith and Nordenfeld, it was not impossible.

A subdued exhilaration which David took to be the fruit of realism, now crept over him. He felt warm. He had dismissed Henry Hammond and lay being rational and grinning in the dark, wondering if he was a quite exceptionally cruel person. He was going to see Dr. Hennessy anyway. He would discuss the matter with him. But will I? None of this sounds really like me, he thought, puffing his pillow, turning on his side, preparing to sleep.

19

'FIRST of all he is going,' said Anne Trematon, 'then he isn't, and now he is, and I'm worried.'

'Boys of that age are secretive. Both mine were.'

'He isn't exactly hiding things, Mrs. Crumm. At least I don't think so. He seems not to know his own mind. I'm not sure what he wants. Sometimes I think he wants the moon. He's—he has become rather silly.'

The older woman shifted sideways into a correct set posture on her own sofa. She had been stroking her legs. Now she stopped and demanded, 'Tell me, dear, what is silly about him?'

'To look at it simply—' Anne began. She stressed 'simply' because she feared something impertinent. She had come to see the husband but he was not back yet, and something told her Mrs. Crumm was on the verge of giving advice, as a married woman for example. 'To look at it simply,' Anne said, 'he is rested and sleeping like a log, but he insists on going back to the doctor after having decided the opposite. He has never been a fusspot about his health. It's not like him to waste his time, his music is everything.'

'Everything?'

'Almost.'

Anne considered for a moment. An intricate and tender shyness was settling on her. She partly shook it off and said, 'He is very talented. Everyone who has taught him, or heard him even, is sure he will be a fine player. Did I tell you, he is a violinist?'

'Like Yehudi Menuhin,' Mrs. Crumm stated comfortably.

'No. He will never be a soloist. He is a string quartet player.' Anne reached out in a quick start of feeling towards her brother. 'They hope to be as good musicians as the Budapest Quartet one day.'

'Oh,' said Mrs. Crumm.

'But different.'

'All boys of that age are secretive,' Mrs. Crumm continued. 'They have emotional difficulties. It passes off again. Puberty,' she said.

Anne told her in some haste, 'At breakfast this morning we had a quarrel. It was about nothing really (yes he *has* got silly) it all arose from me telephoning this doctor of his. You see he went in the first place without telling me he was going, he went on the spur of the moment, I knew he was sleeping badly, and when he came home he showed me his medicine and said he had an appointment to see Dr. Hennessy again when it was finished. He has been sensible taking it. But the other evening when I reminded him he was due to see the doctor today, he said he wasn't going—just like that. He said he wouldn't go inside a hospital again, or think about one, or about doctors, he must settle down to his music. I told him not to be rude and inconsiderate, there was no need to go if he felt really well but he ought to cancel his appointment. Rather than argue with him, I phoned Dr. Hennessy myself from my office and explained David would not be coming.

'The next thing is this morning he has changed his mind and is going after all. He told me at breakfast. When I asked why he got cross. I don't believe he really knows. I suspect he didn't sleep so well last night, but he kept saying he was perfectly fit and would be stopping his medicine anyway, it wasn't that. He kept saying he was going. I had to tell him about cancelling his appointment. He was very angry. He wanted to know exactly what Dr. Hennessy and I had said on the phone. Actually it amounted to nothing, I told Dr. Hennessy my brother was well now and would prefer not to take up any more of his time. David asked was that all? I said yes except I had remembered to thank him for his kindness.

'And then David burst into tears like when he was a little boy, and shouted at me "He isn't kind. He told me we ought to live apart." I tried to calm him. It was no good. Mixed up with his tears he said he would always love me, and I said I would always love him too but the time would come when one of us wanted to be somewhere else. Sooner or later. I said I felt sure Dr. Hennessy didn't mean we ought to separate immediately. But that only made matters worse.'

'Naturally,' said Mrs. Crumm.

Anne waited. Then she asked, 'Why do you say naturally?'

'One comes across many such cases.'

Anne waited again.

'One has to be firm, dear, one must be cruel to be kind. A boy of that type will cling to you if you let him, and the longer you postpone the inevitable day, the closer he will cling.'

Thoughtful and in slight distress, Anne replied, 'David said it wasn't inevitable.'

'The closer he will cling, and the more he will be hurt in the long run.'

'He said why assume anything? Why behave as if a change was going to happen? He said—while he was crying—we were so happy. And we are, Mrs. Crumm.'

'You must miss a life of your own.'

'No I don't,' said Anne carefully.

'With your looks.'

'I should like to travel. I don't want to live in London always.' She's making complicated guesses (thought Anne) about my life, I wish she wouldn't. 'Some day. It would be nice. But I like things as they are.'

'The young men may have other views.'

Or am I the complicated one, Anne began to wonder, while Mrs. Crumm talked about when she was a girl herself, how it was and must be still—'unless the world has changed beyond recognition,' she was saying, when her husband walked in.

The Reverend Crumm said he was sorry he was late. Anne observed his quick and brittle movements, it was as if he meant to catch up. He snatched her hand in a merry way and asked was she cold, had she been waiting long? He was not wearing a parson's collar. And he looked her straight in the eye. She did not believe in his jolliness. She trusted him though.

'It was good of you to see me,' she said, 'at such short notice.'

He waved the thought aside and asked, 'What can I do?'

He looked alert. On the ready. She imagined him carrying a ghostly bag of tools around with him, the means of comfort, and she smiled in the face of her other feelings. She said, 'I have been telling your wife'—but got no further. Mrs. Crumm uttered a kind of summons, exclaiming 'Leo!' He answered 'Yes, Gwen.' She then said, 'You never told me about Miss Trematon's brother.' 'What about him?' 'He came to see you.' 'Yes. Yes he did. He saw me after evensong the Sunday before last. I hope he is all right,' said the Reverend Crumm, turning to Anne.

Later Anne asked herself if she was to blame for her meeting with the Crumms not going better. Being who she was, she was bound to connect mischance in the world around her with some inner fault. Nevertheless, though only for the briefest second, she did intend to seal off the wife, as she turned to face the husband.

She said, 'I think he is all right, thank you. It is hard to be sure with one's own brother. He was over-excited as I expect you noticed, but a doctor gave him some medicine soon after he saw you, and since then he has been much better. Until this morning when it flared up again. You know Mr. Gedge.'

'Do we know Mr. Gedge!' said Mrs. Crumm.

'You know Mr. Gedge. The same doctor who gave David the medicine is looking after Mr. Gedge. David says you hope to find lodgings for him. But I gather,' said Anne, a questioning lift in her voice and her eye on the Reverend

Crumm, 'I gather Mr. Gedge is not well enough to leave hospital yet.'

'No,' said Mrs. Crumm.

'I have been looking in twice a week,' said the husband, 'and I am sure you are right. But whether they will succeed in keeping him there is another matter. He is more and more restless now they have stopped the narcosis treatment.'

'David was talking to someone last night who said they have no legal right to make him stay in hospital against his will.'

'That's not a thing for Gedge to hear,' the Reverend Crumm said quickly, 'a fellow like that, even if it's true.'

'The truth is the truth,' said Mrs. Crumm, standing up.

'Of course, spiritually speaking.'

He stood up too.

Anne said, 'You have both been very kind to him. And to us. David and me. I came to thank you.' She felt uncomfortable still sitting down, and reached for her handbag. 'I mean I'm glad to have the opportunity of thanking you. Actually I came because I promised David I would. He is very anxious Mr. Gedge's time in hospital shouldn't be made longer than necessary because lodgings can't be found for him, and I promised to tell you he can stay with us anyhow for a few days if you haven't found somewhere suitable by the time he comes out. David knows I don't think this is a good idea, we haven't even got a spare room really. But I'm worried about him and I made him promise in return he would be completely frank with the doctor about his funny moods—about everything—when he sees him this afternoon. He had seemed to be so much better. Goodness knows what will happen.' Anne looked down at the handbag in her lap and remembered what it was doing there. 'Another thing,' she said, opening it and taking a cheque-book out, 'I also promised David—I had to—I'm afraid you will call it humouring him, Mrs. Crumm—I promised I would do my best to persuade you to let us

154

pay back the loan you made to Mr. Gedge. David says he is our responsibility more than yours. He got very upset about it this morning. He cried. Oh it seems more than an hour ago.'

The others were still standing.

'You mustn't be offended,' said Anne, 'if I insist. Something small and practical like this, I believe it will help him find his balance. I don't want him to be silly.'

She looked up at the Reverend Crumm and said, 'So I will make out a cheque for ten pounds.'

He replied, 'Can't we think of a better way of being practical?'

His wife laid a hand over the hand that held the cheque-book.

'No, dear. No. If you have ten pounds to spare, find some pretty thing to spend your money on. In any case it was five pounds, not ten. I know all about it.'

'David did say ten. Oh heavens, I wish he wouldn't tell lies.'

Anne raised her head again.

The Reverend Crumm returned her gaze, and said in a voice unlike his own, 'The amount was ten pounds.' At which Mrs. Crumm looked sharply across the room at him and walked out.

20

HENRY HAMMOND was not having an easy morning either. He kept telling himself: He hates me, well at least I can say I know, it's as well to know. Not that he had any idea why it was as well to know. He seemed to have managed better without knowing. He could not concentrate on his work this morning, which was almost unheard of. He sat at his desk. For some reason he did not think about Anne Trematon at all, he wondered what David was doing. (David was in the Royal Academy basement where the lavatories were and old newspapers and shoe-cleaning things, killing time until nearer this afternoon.) But once, late on, when Graham Wilson who shared the room with him said it was stuffy, Henry Hammond threw the window up and stuck out his head to appreciate the air; and this caused him to remember his brother Samuel.

For in very south-east London, beyond Blackheath and Greenwich, Charlton Athletic Reserves were playing an important practice match against the first team. In fact the game was over when Henry Hammond stuck his head out of that window, and Sammy had already bathed in a long trough with the other players, a custom which made him feel blood-brotherly once he was used to it; and he was changed and stood talking to the assistant trainer, who was saying 'It stands out a mile what you need. Experience.' They were on the pitch, on the turf itself. It came as an epic privilege to be pressing the turf not with football boots but walking shoes, and the natural amphitheatre (which is why the ground is called The Valley) rose above them, empty of course but it looks as good as empty with ten thousand gathered there; even when Charlton are drawing big crowds the ragwort flourishes on the higher terraces; and Sammy took in the distant skyline, the trodden green, the stud marks at his feet, while the trainer's voice repeated 'Experience. You're young. You'll learn. You're the type. I watched Cliff Bastin at your age. You're young mind but so was that other bloke, I expect you saw the film. So was Young Mr. Pitt.' 'He must have been when you think,' Sammy answered dreamily. Every bruise on his body sang for joy. Every ache. He longed to tell his parents.

Now they at this moment were quarrelling. It was one of their usual contented quarrels. She was cooking and he sat at the kitchen table. She was telling him to stop moaning, and he replied he wasn't moaning he was putting the record straight. 'You and your talk!' she then said, and they both fell silent. Mr. Hammond was peeling potatoes in a tin basin for tomorrow's Sunday dinner. It was the bottom of the year for the old crop of potatoes, so he was chipping and needling as well as peeling. Slow and careful work. He enjoyed it. Nevertheless he was not quite at peace under one implication of his wife's scolding, and suddenly he said, 'You think I'm all talk and no do. That's what you think. Right.'

It became clear what was in Mr. Hammond's mind when David arrived at the Royal Oak Hospital for Nervous Disorders to keep his appointment that afternoon, and, finding no Dr. Hennessy in the little office, crossed the passage and tentatively opened the door of Alamein Ward.

All was quiet inside, but the hush was intense, gleeful and fragile, like trouble brewing at school. The men in bed—the patients—simply looked at David.

He ventured further in.

He could hear voices in the small annexe beyond, so he followed the sound, and there was Mr. Gedge still in his pyjamas but with socks on and unlaced boots. He was sitting on the drop-side edge of his cot, listening to Dr. Hennessy. Dr. Hennessy was addressing Mr. Hammond.

'This,' he was saying, 'is what happens when idle sods and sea-lawyers like you are given a five-day week. You spend your two free days making it impossible for other people to do any work.'

Frowning and listening, Mr. Gedge reached forward to pick his shirt off the floor, and at that moment the nurse—not Sister Osborne—who was in attendance snatched his suit trousers from underneath him. He had been sitting on them, guarding them.

'There!' she said.

'Nowhere!' shouted Mr. Hammond. 'Or let me tell you where,' he added in much quieter tones. 'To the charge of False Imprisonment will be added the further counts of Detinue of Chattels Personal and Conversion of the same—to the Defendant's use,' he concluded, shifting his angry gaze from the nurse to the doctor.

A pair of heavy winter pants dropped out of the trousers. The nurse swept them up into her arms. But at a sign from Dr. Hennessy she laid her whole burden down again.

He said, 'Without a certificate we can't stop anyone leaving here who wants to. There are good grounds—medical grounds—against applying for a certificate in this case. But if the patient goes before we say he's fit and we hear later he has been a nuisance, you know what to expect.'

David came out with 'He won't be a nuisance.' Some force was taking possession of him and he seemed to be stammering for the first time in his life.

'God almighty! You again!' said Dr. Hennessy. He had not noticed David before. He glared at him now. 'You seem determined to walk straight into trouble.'

'There isn't anything the matter, son?' asked Mr. Hammond.

'There bloody soon will be,' Dr. Hennessy said. 'Who the hell let you in here? I told you to stay away from this one. Unless you want to end up worse that you began.'

With the utmost urgency, as if he were a blazing piece

of paper, David said, 'Listen to me. I will never stay away. You asked me, did I love him—'

'Not quite, laddie,' Dr. Hennessy interrupted in a changed voice. 'I didn't quite say that.' David could feel himself being scrutinised. 'But let's talk about it. I'd like you to find your way back to my office and wait for me. I'll be with you in a minute.'

'—and I betrayed him. I said no. Never, never again. He's going to live with us, in our flat, my sister and I are not separating, you must understand that, I want no more talk about separation. He's going to live with us until he is completely well. We need each other. We all need each other.'

'We do indeed,' said Dr. Hennessy with a wry private smile. Collecting himself, he asked, 'Are you still taking that medicine I gave you?'

'He is coming to live with us. I shan't need it any more.'

Dr. Hennessy repeated patiently, 'Are you still taking it?'

'We will have each other.'

'Oh,' said Mr. Gedge.

They all turned towards his cot, but Mr. Gedge was a bit fat as we know, and he may have said 'Oh' because he was bending over his bootlaces—they all turned his way except Dr. Hennessy who stated directly into David's ear, 'Furthermore, he is a sexual risk. I am warning you.'

21

A few minutes later Mr. Hammond and David were to be
seen downstairs in the main entrance. They made conversation. It wasn't easy. They were waiting for Mr. Gedge.

He would join them very soon, according to Dr. Hennessy.

'I have been here twice before,' David said, looking
round. 'Anyhow,' replied Mr. Hammond, 'it's not my idea of
a hospital.' And he began to do the same.

David was experiencing a mixture of fear and elation.
The purple medicine seemed not to work although he was
still taking it, in fact he had taken a double dose before
coming here. He had three or four days' supply left. Then
it would be finished.

He could not think that far ahead. In so far as his
thoughts had a focus he was remembering the scene in
Alamein Ward. So, apparently, was Mr. Hammond who
now said, 'What did he mean, talking like that, "This is the
end of the road," just as we came away? He was full of
himself, that doctor.'

He was washing his hands of us, thought David. The
very image scared him. But excited him.

'He knows the law, I give him that,' said Mr. Hammond.

At the end, the end of the road, Dr. Hennessy had dismissed the nurse who said 'There!' and a hairy man came
instead, a male nurse to see to the getting dressed, and
separately a lady almoner who handed out a ration book
and identity card, like reprimands, from her safe keeping.
Mr. Gedge said he didn't deserve them. She said 'They are
yours' and asked him a sceptical question, a matter of
form, what was his future address? David intervened to

name Long Acre firmly. 'He's staying with you?' she asked. 'Living with us,' David said. 'You won't buy peace like that,' Dr. Hennessy told him, and David noted *buy* not *find*, and said, 'You think—or do you want me to think?—having Mr. Gedge at home is a bribe, a pretence, it looks unselfish, it's really a way of keeping Anne for myself.' And Dr. Hennessy said, 'I'm no longer very interested, this is the end of the road. I suggest both of you wait downstairs and your friend will join you shortly.'

'He knows the law, and therefore he knows when he is beaten,' Mr. Hammond said.

A picture of the doctor washing his hands was as silly as being frightened by a spoon, David thought for some reason.

'Here he is!' he actually said. Mr. Gedge had appeared on the staircase. These were the Hyde Park clothes, but imposed, laid on him. Gloves. The same vigilant smile. Did someone help him dress? David wondered. Or were they not yet used to being worn again, his clothes?

Mr. Gedge walked down the stairs slowly like entering water.

I don't need to buy peace, David thought, I have it here. There are just two facts. I love my sister and I will not betray my—

Rather than choose a word he looked Mr. Gedge full in the face.

What a beginning! Eye to eye. David introduced Mr. Hammond correctly. Everyone shook hands. It was sober and beautiful. Friend is absolutely the right word, David thought. And all this must lead to work, the work that counts. Music!

'Well?' said Mr. Hammond.

All three looked at each other.

Together, in silence, they left the hum and sour green light of the Hospital for Nervous Disorders.

'Soon I will find my land legs,' said Mr. Gedge.

Mr. Hammond cautioned him to go easy. 'You don't

want to burst your boilers,' he said with a clever glance at David.

'I believe you were a sailor,' David prompted.

Mr. Gedge remained doubtful for a while. Then a change appeared on his lips from far away. He began to speak. It had been fun, he said, the greatest fun, though difficult to get his book written. 'Not impossible,' he added. 'But I failed.'

The sky out here was marvellously aerial.

'You will succeed,' David said.

'That reminds me,' said Mr. Gedge, and he stopped to wind the watch in his waistcoat pocket and count his money. The three of them were under a wall. David told him it was fixed he would live at Long Acre, meaning he must not worry about money or time or anything else. He guessed Mr. Gedge was becoming agitated.

But how wrong he was. Far from being agitated, Mr. Gedge put the others more and more at their ease, talking and explaining things as they strolled along. He dealt with Long Acre first. In royal fashion he declared he was looking forward to his visit. But it must not be prolonged. After a few days his thoughts would be clamouring for elbow room. 'And so will yours,' he said.

David embarked on a polite denial which soon trailed into silence. For he saw the wisdom of Mr. Gedge's words, words expressing the calm scope and sanity of their friendship, and at the same time charming away a fear which David became aware of by that name only when Mr. Gedge spoke and it was gone. Anne had said, 'Asking anyone to live with you—with us—is a serious undertaking, David,' at breakfast during their quarrel. 'Mr. Gedge isn't anyone,' was his reply then. The thing got buried in anger and more talk. It lay buried but sensitive through his miserable empty morning and when the lady almoner asked Mr. Gedge where he was going to live, David felt something jump, not knowing what it was. It might have lodged with him for ever if a wise man had not reached down to exorcise it.

'But we do want you to stay with us. A few days. I don't know. Let's wait and see.' Protesting faintly, David loved his sister for anticipating Mr. Gedge, and admired his friend in the sweet force of his tact, confirming without quite echoing Anne's judgment. And I agree too, he thought: asking anyone to live with you is a serious, a fearful undertaking. But (so his mind strayed on) Mr. Gedge is not anyone, he is special. That is also true.

In his happiness—Mr. Gedge was walking in the middle with Mr. Hammond on his right—David faced sideways towards the others, preparing to say something extraordinarily warm yet rational and the equal concern of all three of them, but not yet clear what it should be.

Mr. Hammond caught his eye.

It was Mr. Gedge who spoke, however. Staring ahead of him, he asked, 'What is your sister's name?' When David told him, he pronounced, 'The simplest names are best,' with such a careworn expression that David felt sure his thoughts had found their way back to his book.

'It seems to me,' David said, 'a name is specially simple when it is the name of something else as well as the person whose it is, like April or Iris—or Dawn, which is the name of Mr. Hammond's daughter.' He was addressing them both together as he had planned. 'It ought to be the other way round,' he said. 'A name which is the name of something else as well ought to be less simple than one which isn't. If you see what I mean.'

'And what about Prudence and Faith?' Mr. Gedge asked, stopping dead in his tracks. He looked sly and expectant, though just as tired as before. He laid his head on his left shoulder. His tongue was visible exactly as when David first set eyes on him in Oxford Street. His tongue did not protrude, one must understand, nor did his mouth gape open though in the nature of things it cannot have been shut.

He seemed to be wondering, Now what will you say to that?

At this moment a single drop of rain struck the pavement

163

as from nowhere. There was no wind. David stood deep in thought.

'Oh I'm enjoying this!' exclaimed Mr. Gedge without really waiting for an answer.

'Hold just one minute,' said Mr. Hammond, because they were beginning to move on again.

'Aren't you enjoying it?' asked Mr. Gedge.

'I want to suggest to our senior partner,' said Mr. Hammond, catching David's eye once more, 'we ought to decide where we are going.'

David saw no such necessity. To be walking away from the hospital was enough. And he would never join a conspiracy to manage Mr. Gedge.

'Because why not have a bite of tea at my place?' said Mr. Hammond. 'There will be just the wife. She won't be surprised to see us. Though she isn't expecting us. Don't misunderstand me. She is open-minded about it, if you like.' And he went on to tell them how he and Mrs. Hammond had been discussing Mr. Gedge this morning; and he, Mr. Hammond, had said, not for the first time, hospitals were disgraceful the way they traded on a patient's ignorance of his legal rights; and she had said, also not for the first time, what was important was to do something.

Another drop of rain fell, smaller than the first but big even so. Then several more.

'It's nice in the sun,' said David, dimly conscious of a prodigy of nature. For the sun did shine, and the raindrops, just these few, fell perfectly straight but must have been carried from a distant bank of cloud over Shepherd's Bush. They must have been brought in from the west on the still air.

David turned the palms of his hands towards the sun. Then he did say, 'And it's raining.'

'The Seventeen bus goes this way,' declared Mr. Hammond who was still waiting for an answer to his invitation, 'and passes my door as near as makes no difference, so nobody need drown.'

'We all have our plans,' said Mr. Gedge.

He suddenly added, 'Did you see me count my money?' He projected the question straight ahead of him, conjuring a spirit of free enquiry.

'The party is on me,' said Mr. Hammond; and he insisted that if Mr. Gedge and David came to Melbourne House they should allow him to pay their bus fares.

Mr. Gedge then asked what would be the cost of a single bus fare from where Mr. Hammond lived back to the Royal Oak Hospital for Nervous Disorders?

Fourpence, Mr. Hammond told him.

Confidence breeds confidence, and David found himself saying at once, almost easily, 'I'm afraid you are hard up.'

On the contrary, Mr. Gedge was all right. He had to be careful, he said. 'I'm all right. I can't complain—but I do sometimes.'

The joke went to David's heart and he did a quick sum. He was working out how much Anne and he could afford to lend. He had a picture of the first few days out of hospital proving awkward financially, even with free board and lodging.

Mr. Gedge, it now transpired, was also doing a sum, though on a smaller scale. Unless prices had changed it should be possible, he told them both, to buy a cup of tea for threepence at a place he used to frequent when he was an outpatient at the hospital. He must return later in the day to collect his book. He had stipulated that it be kept locked in the Dangerous Drugs Safe to which the lady almoner possessed no key, or so she said. Therefore it would be cheaper to buy himself a cup of tea here, where he hoped his friends would join him, rather than accept Mr. Hammond's hospitality.

With quiet dignity Mr. Hammond said one must remember, making these calculations, that more than a cup of tea would be forthcoming at Melbourne House.

Thanking him, Mr. Gedge conceded this point but said he wanted nothing to eat. The place he was thinking of sold buns, though, if the others were hungry.

David's thoughts turned from a substantial loan to a gift of fourpence. The return fare.

Mr. Gedge was saying he could not guarantee the freshness of the buns on a Saturday afternoon.

Try as he might, David found the idea of a gift impossible. He took another run at it in the light of the further consideration that one penny was the significant figure, not four. The difference between the bus fare and the cup of tea. One penny. He tried again. It was still impossible. By now the pavement around them was thickly starred with raindrops. It had been a dry first week of May, and the rising smell of earth which comes so strongly in cities when it does come, was assailing them. David felt a first shiver of wind.

The sun had at last gone in.

'Well?' said Mr. Hammond.

They reached the shelter of Mr. Gedge's shop ahead of a veritable cloudburst. They ran inside. He, Mr. Gedge, asked the girl (who said she was pleased to see him after all this time, and kissed him as it were secondarily) for three cups of tea, and they all then found their seats but left them at once to stand in the window and watch the rain, not falling any longer but beating the ground, thrashing it, until the road formed a watery film and each drop impressed a split-second crater as it struck and vanished. Over the road a fine ferment of spray, very very fine, a haze, a fume, began to hang.

They watched the progress of a cardboard box which the stream was tugging and jostling along the gutter. Mr. Hammond asked Mr. Gedge if this was like a storm at sea. One had to shout because of the noise. The rain set up a continuous drumming boom behind the plate-glass window.

A fly, ignoring the noise outside, landed on the window and rubbed two legs together, and again, the same two, as if sharpening them.

It might sound eccentric, David thought, anyhow finnicky, to measure threepences and fourpences like Mr. Gedge, but only people outside Mr. Gedge's mind would see it that way. The main trouble was having to earn money while he finished his book, that was what led to overworking and a breakdown before, even Henry Hammond recognised that. Mr. Gedge put it in a nutshell himself when he said he must be careful. He's a great man, David determined, recalling the incomplete humour—it was genius—of *I can't complain but I do sometimes*. If I told that to somebody else they would say it was just a game with words, David thought.

And then the girl appeared with their tea. They were alone in the shop except for a taxi-driver. David faced his two older companions at a table for four, planning to make a firm contribution to the subject of Mr. Gedge's book as soon as opportunity served. Their discussion of names had been cut short. He remembered Dawn the girl and suddenly *Blush of Dawn* in Hyde Park, and bits of the Bible, funny things, 'Take thou the pen of a man and write with it concerning Mahashalalhashbaz.' His head was swarming. He also wanted to go back and deal with the fact, if it was quite a fact, anyhow it must not be left untouched, the fact that Mr. Gedge had failed with his book when he was a sailor. No hurry, we've all the time in the world, David told himself, time for the right sort of encouragement—he is coming to stay. For a few days. Wisely. A few is right. And all the more precious.

So Mr. Gedge and Mr. Hammond were engrossed in conversation and David sat opposite them with an empty chair beside him, listening. Of course he was also watching closely.

22

WHAT he saw was Mr. Gedge's hand straying over the table towards the saucerless cup in front of him. He had taken off one glove to drink his tea. Every few seconds his fingers groped forward, they went by feel, his head was turned towards Mr. Hammond. Every few seconds his fingers worked forward over the table-top for contact, but withdrew as soon as they touched the side of the cup. They had been taught a lesson which they proceeded to forget almost at once, groping forward again until they met the sudden heat—and thus the pattern was repeated.

Perfectly natural, thought David, perfectly natural in a philosophic mind. Talk was animated, the tea was much too hot to drink. In truth David scarcely thought about it at all. But he watched the hand. He had never seen a hand of Mr. Gedge's ungloved before. It was fair and small in itself with, however, blighted finger-nails, not bitten but discoloured seriously.

Mr. Hammond was doing most of the talking though Mr. Gedge had started it, mentioning Mr. Hammond's remarks to Dr. Hennessy about legal rights, saying he (Mr. Gedge) was interested in the language and concepts of lawyers: and was it true the difference between libel and slander lay between written and spoken words? 'The law's only a hobby of mine,' Mr. Hammond warned him, he was in marine insurance himself; but with that he presented a masterly account of the matter. Written and spoken words was a common way of expressing it, he said, but the underlying distinction—'the rationale of Defamation'—lay between permanent and impermanent representations.

'Only the permanent can change,' remarked Mr. Gedge.

Mr. Hammond stared at him for a moment and then

described one case in which a gramophone record, and another in which a waxwork figure, were the subject of a libel action. (The likeness of a Moderator of the Church of Scotland had been carried into the Chamber of Horrors by a careless porter, and left there among the famous murderers.)

'Then do we conclude,' said Mr. Gedge, frowning, his hand groping forward yet once more, 'that defamatory sky-writing by an aeroplane, being, although writing, what lawyers would call impermanent—'

'The rain's easing off,' interrupted David whose eyes had been drawn to the window by this last idea.

'Ah!' said Mr. Gedge, relaxing his brow, apparently at ease.

In a single movement he grasped his cup and raised it to his lips.

David had almost no time. The best he could do was to seize his own cup and say 'This is nearly boiling.'

Mr. Gedge took a gulp. And another. He acknowledged David's words with a small toasting gesture, silently.

David then said, 'I couldn't do that.' It sounded utterly feeble. He was flustered. He couldn't say 'Are you mad?' or even 'Stop!' At least *he* couldn't say 'Stop!'

So he said 'I couldn't do that.'

'Very few can,' replied Mr. Gedge. 'Very, very few can.' And he drank the rest of his tea.

Belatedly Mr. Hammond said, 'Easy, easy.'

But by now Mr. Gedge was looking out of the window himself. An austere light entered his face, suggesting a return to the sky-writing aeroplane or some similar problem.

David studied him with a heavy heart. He thought of nervous disorders and scalding tea. He pictured Dr. Hennessy washing his hands. He imagined him bending over a basin of dreadful outcomes which were no longer his care and medical duty, inspecting his wholesome nails, scrubbing and rinsing.

So what! But so what! David was thinking by the time his tea was cool enough to drink.

Mr. Gedge produced this change single-handed. Out of the blue. He swung away from the window and the dwindling rain, and turned on David and demanded, 'Why aren't you working?'

'I should be,' David said.

The directness of this was wonderful, it was immediately liberating. Instead of the internal fret, to himself, against himself: drinking boiling tea must be sinister—but suppose it's just physical—a philosopher's dog once chewed his foot off while he was lost in thought, or so Hans Neumann told us—and then the next physical thing might be, well, more serious, sex is physical Dr. Hennessy would say—

Instead, all was shattered only to be drawn into a single sheaf, a soft knot, inescapable.

He loves me, David thought, as I do him, as friends should. Being the much older friend he rebukes the other, me that is, not harshly, but not sentimentally, understanding his talent without letting him see too much. And the other, me, of course, must study philosophy and encourage and criticise and not mind but step forward calmly if everyone else calls the older friend mad.

23

A PARTY took place on the third which was to be the last but one day of Mr. Gedge's visit.

The occasion was carefully thought out. He was leaving the next afternoon. Wack and Hans Neumann and Colin Innes came to supper; with Mr. Gedge and Anne and David that made six, the largest number ever to sit down together in the flat. The quartet had all eaten there before, of course, though very seldom at the same time and never with anybody from outside.

The fact was noted by Hans Neumann.

'I wish to congratulate our hostess,' he announced over the coffee.

'I say too. Absolutely. But with no pomp. I am sincere,' said Wack. He had already complimented Anne—he always did—on her ice cream.

Mr. Gedge and Colin Innes were talking about Scotland, the school system. Colin must have heard the sort of thing that was being said elsewhere at the table; he looked up at Anne with his positive glance and remarked, 'I'm busty full, I liked it,' as if he were alone with her.

'And,' Hans Neumann went on, 'I salute a true student of chamber music, an admirer of the Flonzaley.'

He bowed towards Mr. Gedge.

Earlier in the evening Mr. Gedge had surprised and delighted them—had made them cluster round him so to speak—by enquiring, Why was the Flonzaley Quartet not better known in England?

That was a real question. 'In England! In Europe let us say! Why not in Europe, we may ask to ourselves?' Wack had enlarged vehemently. It was a proud moment. My friend, David thought. Anne seemed to feel it too.

'The Flonzaley!' Mr. Gedge responded now, at the end of the meal, across the table to Hans Neumann. He raised his cup. He made as if to toast those fine players. The coffee was still too hot to drink, and David experienced his first distinct fear since they arrived together on Saturday afternoon, early evening rather, three days before, and Anne, waiting to meet and welcome Mr. Gedge at the head of the stairs, said, 'How nice of you to come; I'm so glad to hear that you are well again,' and he answered merely, 'Again?'

'Again?' was disconcerting.

Thereafter all had been peaceful and cordial.

It was strenuous though. As Mr. Gedge restored his cup of coffee to its saucer, untasted, safe, and Hans Neumann denounced the policies of 'your' gramophone companies—'*Kunstpoliti*k makes reputations and fame. *Kunstpolitik*. There is no English word'—David recognised that this visit had been certainly not too long, but long enough. Mr. Gedge had judged it right. His prompt and whimsical ways, much to be prized in an older friend, were tiring to live with. 'Again?' was no joke if you considered it properly, it was as real as the Flonzaley Quartet. In fact it was too real, like being aware of all the accidents that might happen to you at any time. Even when Mr. Gedge wasn't asking questions, he was doing that as well as whatever he was doing, there was a question at the bottom, or rather there was no bottom and no proper sides either, your head felt in a draught with him. It was a strain.

It was also very happy. Mr. Gedge borrowed David's room and David slept in the kitchen; he and Anne resurrected a first-war camp-bed from the family luggage, and he practised in the evenings in her room which she hardly ever used between tea and supper. It was a good arrangement but it would not be practical for very long, David realised, and he meant to admit to Anne that she had been right about this during their quarrel. He would tell her when Mr. Gedge left them. But Mr. Gedge could not have been a more discreet guest. He went to bed early the first night, and the second day, his first full day, he worked non-stop. They scarcely knew he was there.

He was obviously tired that second evening, having worked all day. He held his head lightly in his hand. David offered him an aspirin which he accepted, he said he hadn't got a headache but in case there was pain around. The three of them chatted for a while. David was waiting for a chance to talk about Mr. Gedge's book. Then there happened to be a silence, and in it could be heard the small insect-noise of a watch being covertly wound, and David saw Mr. Gedge's fingers, in cotton gloves as always, dipped inside his waistcoat pocket. He urged him not to stay up if he was ready for bed.

'I believe I am ready,' Mr. Gedge said, but the only way to be sure was to go and lie down—and he disappeared.

He returned almost at once holding a screw of paper. He said he had noticed a bundle of kitchen rubbish being carried downstairs after supper.

David drew back the curtain and led him down to the stone steps and down again to the basement, and showed him the boiler fire.

'This is where I burnt your hat,' David said on a sudden impulse. 'I never told you.'

In his different way Mr. Gedge showed the same lack of interest as Dr. Hennessy. He said he was coming on a similar errand himself, and while they watched the paper burn he said that part of bracing himself for a fresh attack on his book first thing tomorrow morning, was to cut his toe-nails.

Thus David got his chance to discuss the so-called failure of the book at that earlier stage, when Mr. Gedge was a sailor.

He learnt many things that were new to him. Mr. Gedge began by describing a big battleship where he had been in charge of the library. It was a simple job which left him plenty of time for his writing, and Mr. Gedge had made it simpler still by scrapping the author and title catalogues (with the agreement, the positive encouragement, he said, of the other sailors) and dividing the entire stock of books into Cowboys and Spicy Stories. An officer who wished him ill presented the ship's library with a complete Hazlitt. Mr. Gedge ruled that the *Liber Amoris* and the second volume of the *Life of Napoleon* were spicy, and the rest was cowboys. The officer appealed to the captain who said that the ship's librarian's decision was final.

Everything to do with Mr. Gedge and the navy seemed so long ago, David asked him when and how it all started. A lot was now explained. You could become a sailor at the age of fifteen in those days, which Mr. Gedge did. You were a Boy Seaman and as well as learning navigation and signalling, boxing the compass, splicing and cheesing down ropes, manning the whaler, being smart aloft, making Turk's Heads, practising bends and hitches at a jack-stay— as well as being a sailor you did ordinary reading, writing and arithmetic under instructor officers known as Schoolies. They taught the school subjects. The only exception was religion which the Chaplain taught.

Mr. Gedge could read already when he joined the navy, his mother was a chemist's daughter. He had a start over the other boys and the Schooly lent him books which he got interested in, and that was how his own book began. 'It must have been hard,' David said with an eye to some forceful encouragement when he had heard a bit more. 'It must have been very hard considering all the other things you had to do.' 'Difficult but not impossible,' Mr. Gedge replied. It would have been *very* difficult if he had remained a Seaman. But he became a Sailmaker. The change was suggested by his Schooly. Sailmakers did not make sails any more, there were no sails to make, but the name stayed the same. That was like the navy. It was one of the things that set Mr. Gedge thinking about names. In modern times Sailmakers were odd-job men, and the important thing was they had a tiny cabin to themselves to keep their tools in. There was only one Sailmaker to a ship. The top of the tool-locker made an excellent desk and one could empty a drawer of the locker for books. Life was hardly ever busy for Sailmakers except in wartime, and then only in short bursts, after an action when they were required to effect any small temporary repairs and to stitch the dead into their hammocks for burial at sea. But then in wartime the bigger ships carried two Sailmakers. In some ways war was quieter than peace. Mr. Gedge was saying, did David realise that in wartime a battleship carried five doctors, all idle, when Anne appeared and laughed at them both—she had begun to wonder where they were—for standing by the smelly hot boiler when they could be comfortable upstairs.

They laughed too and followed her up and finished their talk by the open kitchen window, David's bedroom for the time being and of course it had the bath in it as well, but it was a big room. They leaned against the window-sill and David thought this is the end of our second day, as happy as our first, what there was of our first—and while they stood and chatted he was also recalling showing Mr. Gedge round the flat when they very first arrived together, the eloquence of all things, witnesses of two full years between brother and sister, in his friend's presence at last: shapes and pressures of door-handles each turning with its own voice and character to the hand, points of wear in carpets, stains on walls, cracks over ceilings some right across and some with beginnings like rivers, all known, and glass bubbles and flaws in the windows. The flat smelt very, very faintly of bananas, David always thought. He had a thing about smells. When he took Mr. Gedge into Anne's room there was a small branch, a sprig, of lilac on the dressing-table. He asked Mr. Gedge had he noticed lilac began to smell like a gas leak after a bit, and Mr. Gedge exclaimed 'White lilac!' and approached it on tiptoe in its slender vase, before replying it was the water that smelt. He admired the curtain in the hall—where they ate—and specially the large brass rings. He drew the curtain across and back

175

again exactly as David had imagined him doing. Then David showed him his own things all in order: violin, music, books, certificates and prizes, a scholarship award signed by Sir Percy Allen, his plaster bust of Mozart, he told him how Wack drawled 'Mozart' and Hans Neumann's quite different way of saying it, though they both spoke German. Recklessly he told Mr. Gedge that the quartet was studying Beethoven 127. Their secret. But he said nothing about the other three coming to supper, though this was already fixed.

Nor did he tell him the next night at the kitchen window, a dark night laden with clouds. From where he stood David identified the street-lamp he was sick under before their first meeting. Everything that had happened since then felt meant now. Not inevitable quite but meant. Even the one thing that did not happen according to plan felt meant. He had decided to play the unaccompanied Bach partitas to Mr. Gedge in three private but entirely formal concerts, one on each day of his visit, at a high standard, a celebration. Nothing of the sort took place. It was impossible. When Mr. Gedge reached for his brief-case at the end of being shown round the flat—they finished naturally in David's room which was to be his room—when he took out his book, held his book, it was impossible. David saw at once and accepted, saying 'You will want to work and I must practise,' and the impossibility also felt meant now, at the kitchen window.

In their shared silence David said, 'I can't imagine what it's like being a philosopher.'

'Very few can,' replied Mr. Gedge, 'very, very few can, particularly now. There *are* some philosophers but they can't imagine what it's like. That's why they talk about doing philosophy and not about being philosophers. And many who can't even do philosophy talk like that because Wittgenstein does. They roam in a gang and read papers to each other, asking "Since the world's a blind beggar, shall we say it has real glass eyes or glass real eyes?"'

'Instead of what?'

'Lending a hand or sparing a copper or teaching the world to see with real but glass oh but real eyes. Or quenching the whole blind beggar metaphor. Don't you go near a university,' Mr. Gedge said suddenly. The thought must have come upon him in a rush. He looked appalled. Then, by an extraordinary coincidence (for David was still peering out at the warm yellow nimbus of his street-lamp), one of those chances which seem to occur more often than they should, Mr. Gedge said: 'That's where mind consults its vomit.'

'Music at universities is very bad, they say,' answered David, while he wondered about people, specially friends, reading each other's thoughts. Uncanny. But what an advantage when it comes to helping and encouraging!

'Still,' he went on, 'the university professors have more free time to write their books than you ever had to write yours. You must remember that when you feel depressed.'

'Must I? Today I would like to forget. I have had as much time as any professor.'

'Today is only one day.'

'I failed again.'

'You talked about failing when we were leaving the hospital on Saturday afternoon. You said you had failed to write your book when you were a sailor. But when we first met in Hyde Park you *had* written it. I know you aren't satisfied with it. But you have written it. You haven't failed. You aren't failing. Perhaps it's too early to talk about succeeding. I'm not sure. I am sure you are improving.'

'The Russian for to improve is to make successes. *Dyelat oospyechi*. Say it after me. *Dyelat oospyechi*. Go on.'

'*Dyelat oospyechi.*'

'Again.'

'*Dyelat oospyechi.*'

'Again.'

'*Dyelat oospyechi*. Why is your book called the Russian for sausage?'

177

'Because it is also the Hebrew for All Flesh. Once more.'
'*Dyelat oospyechi.*'
'And once more. Make a meal of it, munch your words.'
'*Dyelat oospyechi.*'
'But if I am making successes, my dearest child, my
pretty, how can I be improving? Or failing? How can I?'

24

So Mr. Gedge still did not know about the party.

'You tell him,' David said to Anne on his way to bed, and she did so next morning, the day it was going to happen.

'I say!' His eyes flashed from one to the other almost as if he suspected a trick. 'You two! oh I say!'

'It's in your honour,' David explained. 'We hope you like it. It's only supper.'

And Mr. Gedge went away to work.

'I'm excited,' he said that evening, emerging stealthily from his, that is David's, room, shooting his cuffs and eyeing the splendid table. 'Those twisty bread rolls. Why do they shine? They remind me. You can't imagine.'

'I hope it's nice,' said David; 'at any rate it will give you a change from philosophy, being with musicians.'

'A change for philosophy, not from it. There are no holidays,' Mr. Gedge replied.

Then David made a calculated remark. He said, 'Staying with the Reverend Crumm will seem more like being with another philosopher, I expect.'

David said this because he wanted more information about Mr. Gedge's plans when he left Long Acre tomorrow. All he knew was he was not going into lodgings but had arranged to stay with the Crumms after all—or rather, with the Reverend Crumm. When David said 'the Crumms', Mr. Gedge corrected him. That was after leaving hospital on Saturday, after the rainstorm. They had gone their separate ways from the shop that sold tea and buns, and when they met again two hours later on the steps of the National Gallery according to plan, so that they could arrive at the flat together, Mr. Gedge announced between breaths he had spoken to the Reverend Crumm and all was well. David wanted to know what all meant. That was why he made his calculated remark. Then he studied his friend, and proceeded, 'He must have been surprised to see you out of hospital.'

Mr. Gedge answered slowly and heavily, unlike talking, more like building, as if he had been drawn back into his day's work, away from the very close party.

'Surprised? You could say his face looked stern, mistrustful, displeased, authoritarian, but surprised only in the manner of a baby that has heard itself break wind and can't locate the noise or find a cause but feels responsible. I am rewarded by the faces of babies and good men, to the point of contemplating a whole new section *On the Face*. That clergyman felt fearfully responsible when he opened his front door to me, and yet I saw no fear in his face. Then what are we to say? We are not always disconcerted by people not looking like what they are, or looking like what they are not. We observe that gynaecologists look like women's hairdressers, and there is nothing here that needs explaining. *On the face of it*. But it is equally true that dentists look like royal chauffeurs. And this, we say, is strange. We grope for a bond between the occupations, and in doing so we remember Kierkegaard's knight of faith who looks like a tax-collector. I am uneasy about Kierkegaard. If he meant the knight of faith is unrecognisable, he should have said so. And I would answer: unrecognisable certainly as a knight (it would be no good accosting someone who looked like a tax-collector, he might be a tax-collector) but detectable in his faith, by the light and cold bonfire scar together of art—in this case the art which theologians call grace and which, being art, and themselves being conventional, they oppose to nature. We detect the knight of faith as we detect the angel who lives behind Rembrandt's eyes. That's why I took you inside the National Gallery. We looked at him carefully, you and I. But we could not recognise him in the street, and we would not even know whom to ask for. Is he the angel of our entire humanity? Or is he the Dutch bourgeois angel? Or is he the angel of certain even more confined morose probities? Or narrower still, must he have a bottle nose and grey curls you long to puff the air through they are so there? Indeed must he have little piggy eyes? We know what we have detected but never whom to ask for, we philosophers of naming, and it is no doubt an accident of my imagination that the thing I find hardest to conceive of here is a teetotal and not a drinking angel, when perhaps I ought to be searching the temperance hotels. Shakespeare spoke for all western men when he complained there's no art to find the mind's construction in the face, that is one reason for learning Russian, and the Americans are even worse at the human face than we are. Henry James writes "Her eyes were what is vulgarly called brown". What is the unvulgar word for brown?'

'I was going to ask *you* a question,' said David at last. 'I know you don't know but why do you think the Reverend Crumm was afraid?'

25

LUCKILY, since Mr. Gedge had fallen under a spell and was in no mood to meet anyone, especially for the first time— luckily nobody came just then. And afterwards this also felt meant, meant rather than luck, that Mr. Gedge should be ready with a handshake and pertinent greeting as he most decidedly was when Colin Innes arrived.

But while his question about the Reverend Crumm went unanswered, David could not be confident. He feared for the success of the evening. Anne, the quartet, and Mr. Gedge. The others would be deeply interested once they were used to him, but he must be disposed to meet them first.

The practical solution was to repeat the question word for word.

'I know you don't know but why—'

'I know I do know,' said Mr. Gedge. 'When he opened the door to me I named his fear with biblical certainty. I was Adam when God brought things to him to see what he would call them.'

'I remember. The second chapter of Genesis. And whatever Adam called each thing, that was the name thereof.'

'God's vulgar curiosity must not be mistaken for the metaphysical ardour of the philosopher of naming, and neither must Adam's compliant dogmatism. With God smirking beside him Adam should have said "Over to you, this isn't man's work".'

'Well he didn't say that. Nor did you. You named the Reverend Crumm's fear.'

'But with no God beside me. So I couldn't say "Over to you", I could only name and think and go on thinking. I am a man of no faith, you see, but of compelling scriptural memories.'

'Like me,' said David. 'We had the Bible read to us when we were little. I can scarcely remember. Anne was bigger. Music is my religion now,' he said, and planted his gaze in Mr. Gedge's eyes.

Mr. Gedge answered, 'So that's what you call it. Tell me again.'

'My religion.'

'Again.'

'My religion.'

Mr. Gedge listened with his head on one side.

Then he said, 'I can hear the creaking of the will. You are a naming animal like the rest, but you are also a very conscious child. I love you for it.'

'I love you too. We've both got brown eyes did you realise. We must be practical,' David said, 'like the best sort of friends. And that's why I keep on asking you about the Reverend Crumm. In some ways I feel older than you. Now tell me why he was afraid.'

After that they were extremely practical. 'It's your future, you must think about it, you must tell me,' David urged him, and Mr. Gedge came back inside ordinary life at once. He said the Reverend Crumm had enough difficulties without seeing him on the doorstep. This sounded common sense. When David prompted him by mentioning Anne's impression of Mrs. Crumm, he refused to be drawn further, he said we all live as we can, and explained there was a disused potting-shed at the bottom of the rectory garden. 'A long Victorian garden,' said Mr. Gedge, pausing, 'big for a town garden.' Plans were afoot to find him cheap lodging in the parish, but they could not be carried out immediately. 'I had—he said I had jumped the gun rather, walking out of hospital.' In the meantime the potting-shed was at Mr. Gedge's disposal.

'You must promise to stay here longer if you want to. Anne and I—'

'Three days is right. We both know. I shall hate leaving you.'

Colin Innes called 'What's cooking? Is anyone at home?' from three-quarters up the stairs.

'And I'm excited for this evening,' Mr. Gedge added softly. He ungloved his right hand and strode to the head of the stairs. 'I am Henry Gedge the philosopher,' he told Colin. 'You would never guess.'

26

STRING players and pianists keep their hands out of really hot water if they can, just as they don't carry suitcases. That is why you see elderly conductors heavily laden and strong young instrumentalists walking beside them carrying nothing.

At Long Acre, on ordinary evenings, Anne used to go straight to the sink when the supper things were stacked and start washing them. David dried for her. The same was true when they weren't alone; she could keep up with two or even three because of the talking. The more the slower was a well-known joke. She got cross about it sometimes when she was tired.

Mr. Gedge and David had been efficient driers yesterday and the day before. Somehow they were good at talking and drying simultaneously. This surprised David and impressed him, he counted it among the favourable omens of their friendship, and he asked himself would it last if there were many more days together, actually living together.

Tonight, nevertheless, he and Anne had decided not to wash up in a crowd of six, but to wait until the other three had left and then say to Mr. Gedge: the party was in his honour, he would have a long tiring day tomorrow with his move to Finchley. Why not go to bed now and leave it to us?

He needed an example in not overworking, in being quiet.

Perhaps Anne foresaw confusion with six.

Anyhow this idea was overturned by Wack. They had all helped carry through to the kitchen. David was folding the hall table and pushing it to one side, so there would be room to sit. The rest of them were in the kitchen stacking dishes. There was a lot of noise. Above the noise David heard Wack say commandingly, 'It must be so. Do not arg me, Flower of London.' Then there was a moment's comparative quiet, and Wack added, again loud and clear, 'Queen of London!' and much laughter followed.

David went into the kitchen and found that Anne had been crowned with one of those crinkly paper decorations which used to surround pie dishes. She was slightly flushed. Dear God, she looked beautiful. Wack was insisting that the washing up be done at once, and that Anne have no part of it. Hans Neumann would wash. 'Cellists cannot be harmed, this is well known,' said Wack—referring to the pretence based upon Casals's square coarse hands and pipe, that cellists are a special class of self-improved peasant.

And so they did wash up, and Anne sat with her paper crown on her knee and joined in the conversation when she felt like it.

If one were to generalise about supper and the time afterwards, it might sound as if Mr. Gedge did most of the talking. But no. For a while it was true he spoke a lot. That was because David in his nervousness virtually forced subjects upon him. He began with Rembrandt, telling the others that he and Mr. Gedge had visited the Dutch room of the National Gallery to look at the late self-portrait. He made Mr. Gedge talk about Rembrandt, and Rembrandt's old age, which led to Franz Hals who also did some of his very best work when he was old, according to Mr. Gedge. David was proud of his friend of course, as well as nervous. 'And then there is Titian painting his heart out in his eighties,' Mr. Gedge was saying. 'It *is* encouraging. Oh it is,' he added, but half inaudibly because Wack was already striking in with 'Verdi! His best work is old I should say. Very old.'

'The Greek tragical author Sophocles also,' said Hans Neumann slowly.

Anne laughed and asked, 'Why turn on the Brains Trust when there's us to listen to?' She searched the faces round the table in her happiest way. The food was nice. 'And we aren't being paid!' she exclaimed. 'Did you see what Osbert Lancaster said about the people in the British Council and Arts Council and all those other new things? He called them salaried culture hounds.'

As if answering her, Mr. Gedge said, 'I am forty-eight, you see, and have scarcely begun.'

She made a motion of denial.

'Not that one wants to be a long time dying.'

'No,' she said.

'Isn't one hard to please!'

'I have done a sum,' said Colin Innes with characteristic suddenness. 'We are seventy-nine. We have scarcely begun either, the quartet hasn't even got a name, and our age together is seventy-nine.'

Relentless in his anxiety to drive the conversation back to where he knew his friend was strong, and despite the fact that Mr. Gedge was showing immediate interest in the quartet's lack of a name, David proclaimed 'Titian!' and when he had secured a pause he asked about the colour of Titian hair, and back further still to vulgar and unvulgar browns and even Henry James. That was how for a while Mr. Gedge came to talk more than anyone else. Only for a while. Not that the others would have been bored if he had gone on longer, he knew so much but not like a professor, and although he had actually mentioned his age he did not seem old. This early part of the evening was when David heard him say 'the china-painter's tones, the Renoir bloom' and many other things he remembered afterwards, and used later in his life, always causing himself pain when he did so.

But then the party settled down and they became equal in every way, David felt, all of them except Anne who could not be compared.

They discussed possible names for the quartet. It was a thing the four of them enjoyed talking about when hopes ran specially high; and tonight, with Anne and Mr. Gedge joining in, and on from there to established quartets—

hence the Flonzaley—and their names, nothing could have been better. They were back in the hall, the washing up finished. By now Mr. Gedge must have been able to picture their lives in considerable detail. Everything to do with their music. It would set a seal on the evening, David suddenly realised, to make a confession. And he did. Looking at Mr. Gedge, he told the other three and Anne that he had entrusted him with the secret of Beethoven 127.

This caused no great stir. They rather assumed Mr. Gedge would know, and Wack also took it for granted he would come at least next Sunday and hear them; saying simply 'I suppose'—meaning I expect—'you admire this work;' and when Mr. Gedge replied yes, Wack warned him that their own study of it was not far advanced. Whereupon Mr. Gedge related the story of 127's first performance, how beforehand Beethoven made fat Schuppanzigh's quartet sign a document pledging them to do their best. And how, after a fiasco—'not their fault,' said Mr. Gedge quickly, the parts reached them late, they were under-rehearsed—Beethoven handed the work over to Bohm's quartet and supervised them himself, crouching in a corner, able to hear nothing but watching their fingering and every movement of their bows.

'Very queer,' said Colin Innes at his most thoughtful and therefore most Scotch.

Hans Neumann likewise doubted if much could be done by look alone.

Wack asked, himself how serious a string player was the composer? a good deal depended on that question.

Nobody knew.

'In any case you can't watch four at once,' said Mr. Gedge after a pause, darting his head from one to the other to prove the point.

'That's why he crouched in a corner of the room,' said Anne, 'to see as much as he could.'

There were many other examples of how lively Mr. Gedge was and altogether sound during the evening.

27

HE was more subdued now, though not exactly unlively. They were all quieter without realising it, getting sleepy, talking about music but really coming to rest in its shadow. Except Anne perhaps. When Wack gave his watch-face a quick frank stare and observed 'We are too late,' she did not say she agreed but David thought she looked tired rather than sleepy.

She said goodbye at the top of the stairs and Mr. Gedge and David trooped down with the others to see them out.

At the street door, just outside, David found himself close to Wack. He said into his ear, 'Some people think he's mad. He isn't, is he?'

Wack considered for a moment before answering quite loudly, 'Absolutely no. He is scholastic but he is a man of feeling.' Then louder still, to Mr. Gedge, 'On Sunday, after music, will you share our large customary meal?'

Mr. Gedge refused, explaining that he never tried to work on a full stomach.

'A body must eat,' said Colin Innes wonderingly, and with that they all bade each other good night. Hans Neumann asked as an afterthought where could one read about 127 being directed by sight alone, it was incredible, and Mr. Gedge said he would bring a book with him on Sunday. He had taken the measure of Hans Neumann. He told him that the standard biography of 'our' Beethoven was by an American, but there existed a competent German translation.

He and David stood on the pavement and watched the others out of sight.

'Do you know the stars?'

This feels meant beyond anything in our three days,

David thought, meant and best, tilting his face in answer towards the sky. His mind tingled at the utter clearness of it. Meant and best. He remembered that Dr. Hennessy's wife, according to Dr. Hennessy, would agree (if she knew about it) that coming to hear the quartet at its ordinary routine practice was the best way to stop Mr. Gedge overworking. And he was coming. Of course Mrs. Hennessy was right. Or rather, she would be right, David corrected himself, smiling.

To Mr. Gedge, on the very verge of teasing him, he said, 'Do you mean, can I *name* the stars?'

Mr. Gedge said nothing.

David looked down and saw he was being gazed at.

Mr. Gedge touched his shoulder and said, 'You are. Yes, you are a very conscious child.'

'I can recognise the Plough,' David said. 'But it doesn't seem to be in sight.'

'Which direction is north, my silly?'

'I've never thought.'

'Then start now.'

'There.'

'No, there. The Plough lies behind this building. We must cross over to see it.'

Anne! came and went in a flash, she's tired, she's waiting for us.

In fact they stopped in the middle of the road. Mr Gedge caught David's arm again and pointed straight overhead to indicate the constellation Cygnus the Swan, neck stretched out, two wings, a short stumpy tail; he picked out each star in turn and told him the Swan was the truest cruciform in the whole sky, much truer than the Southern Cross. The Southern Cross was a crooked little object, not worth a journey to the Mediterranean. 'Oh I say,' he interrupted himself, 'you won't often see the great nebula in Andromeda as plain as that.' He pointed again.

'Which is Andromeda?'

Mr. Gedge drew him silently across the road.

'Now,' he said. 'You know the Plough. So show me the Pole Star.'

'There.'

'No, that's Vega. Vega will do. Take a line—isn't this fun —a line from Vega to the Swan's tail. That's right. The Swan's tail is called Deneb. You've got your line from Vega to Deneb. Now carry on, produce it as they say, go on, veering north—that way—a little. No, you've gone too far, that's Cassiopeia, Andromeda's mother, a ragged W, more like a chair tipped backwards. Back again. That's right, that's Andromeda, there's her head—and up again for her tummy. And that cluster of small stars is her right arm. She's chained on her rock, you see, and there's Perseus at her feet coming to the rescue.'

'There's her left hand.'

'No, that star is in Pegasus. But let's borrow it for to-night. We will give her a left hand. Poor girl. Just for to-night.'

Anne!

Andromeda. The nebula in Andromeda was a faint al-most shapeless stain soaking through the bright stars of that constellation. Mr. Gedge said it was the most distant thing in the universe for the naked eye, before there were tele-scopes.

'How far away?'

'Seven hundred and fifty thousand light-years. Everything we see going on there happened three-quarters of a million years ago.'

They both looked.

'Stale news?' said Mr. Gedge wistfully. 'Stale views? No wonder Philosophy has wanted to play at God and make the world young again as well as known.'

David allowed his sight to roam over the entire visible sky.

'If you don't believe in God,' said he, 'why do you talk so much about him?'

'Do I? Or do I mean don't I? Having no faith is not the

same as disbelief, nor will it be the same as doubt when my great work is done.'

There was a pause. A long pause.

'All the same, I wish you would show me the Southern Cross one day.'

'We will do the next best thing,' said Mr. Gedge at once. 'Come in here.' He led David into the entrance of a shop or office, it was too dark to be sure, and turned round with his back flat against the door.

'Good!' he said. 'We can see the whole Plough from here.'

David's thought was Anne! but Mr. Gedge had begun a lesson on the circumpolar stars. The next best thing to a journey together to see the Southern Cross was to learn about the stars which revolve round the Pole, first the ones which were below the horizon at this time of year but would come up and over with winter. 'That's why we start with Polaris the Pole Star,' said Mr. Gedge, and he went on to show how Polaris can always be found from the Pointer of the Plough. 'But I specially want you to learn a winter constellation. Just one. The Lion. Then when the weather gets colder and he appears, you will think of tonight.'

'And our time together,' said David.

'Next winter. And the one after. And the one after.'

'Every winter. I won't forget ever.'

'And after I'm dead.'

'I can't bear to think of you dying.'

'It will get borne. God will be the absent hero of that story too.'

'We must be sensible,' said David. 'We will see each other on Sunday. That's only six days away. And every night between now and then I will come outside at bed-time and find the Swan and Andromeda if it's a clear night, and then I will cross over here and get my bearings from the Plough and find the Pole Star, and I will laugh when I remember I thought Vega was the Pole Star until you showed me. I

will look at them both and think of you. If Vega is a circumpolar star I can do that any night of the year. I will
feel close to you however far apart we are, as close as
blind friends in the same room. Is Vega a circumpolar star?'

Mr. Gedge was not absolutely sure. You might have to
get out on the roof to see her when she was at her lowest
in the northern sky. You could make certain of Vega by
going to live in Scotland.

They laughed together.

'I will always live in London,' said David, 'because of the
quartet and Anne. And you.'

His 'Anne' reminded him once more. This time he spoke.
He said she would be getting worried, they ought to go
back.

'Leo the Lion. I haven't described our winter constellation.'

'We can do that indoors.'

'So,' said Mr. Gedge. And he turned sideways. Now they
were facing. They stood still. David heard the words 'My
David' and shut his eyes although it was dark in there already. There was movement. They half blundered into
each other and half embraced. One of them, perhaps both,
retreated a little, out of contact. It seemed they were on the
point of leaving that dark doorway. David felt his hand
being prised open and a kiss planted in the palm.

He kept his eyes shut.

His fingers were being folded for him over the kiss.

Anne!

Instantly his world turned blood-suffused. A torch shone
upon his closed eyes, and a voice directed, 'Come out of
there. Both of you.'

They came out.

It was less dark on the pavement. When his eyes began
to work properly David made out a figure in uniform, police
he realised, and somebody else, hatless, also a man.

'I have reason to believe,' the policeman said, 'that a
criminal offence has been committed or contemplated.'

'We were watching the stars,' said Mr. Gedge.

In a less official voice the policeman asked, then why were they hiding?

'We weren't hiding,' said David—and 'Oh that's easy!' came simultaneously from Mr. Gedge who now gave a short and clear account of the Pole Star in relation to those stars in the constellation Ursa Major which are commonly called the Plough or Charles's Wain. The essential fact was that the Pointer of the Plough, from which one learnt to find the Pole Star, otherwise Polaris, could not be seen by anyone standing on the pavement, it was obscured by the roof opposite. But it came into sight if one retired a few yards into a doorway.

The policeman declined Mr. Gedge's invitation to see for himself. Changing his tack, he said they were not watching the stars when he surprised them with his torch.

'No,' said David. 'We were saying goodnight.'

The policeman then spoke of their posture. He asked them to explain their posture. What connection was there between that posture and saying goodnight? He scarcely waited for an answer but shone his torch up and down David's trousers. As so often, a button was undone.

The days before zip flies.

'This person's dress is not correctly adjusted,' said the policeman. He turned to his silent companion. 'Sir, I call on you to witness the fact.'

The man shifted perceptibly in the dark and cleared his throat.

He said, 'I do not know whether I shall be prepared to give evidence.'

'In due course I must ask you, sir, for your name and other particulars.'

'My name is Hammond,' said the man. 'Henry Hammond.'

28

'It's you,' said David.

'Ah, David!' said Henry Hammond. 'You said "It's you" last time we met. That occasion was a surprise too—for both of us.'

Mr. Gedge asked to be introduced.

Henry Hammond ignored him, but turned to the policeman and said, 'Officer, by an extraordinary coincidence it transpires that I know both these gentlemen, the young one and the older one whose health is not good. I expect you would like me to make a formal statement.'

The policeman marshalled them under a lamp-post.

'But perhaps I should make it clear at the outset, though I find the subject embarrassing,' said Henry Hammond, 'that the coincidence is not quite as extraordinary as it seems. When I arrived earlier tonight I was well aware that Mr. Trematon, the younger gentleman, lived here. But I did not expect to meet him, let alone under these circumstances.'

'There's nothing wrong with the circumstances,' David said, also addressing the policeman. 'We have told you the truth. We were saying goodnight. My friend had been teaching me the stars.'

'And we love each other,' added Mr. Gedge.

David steeled himself and said, 'That is true too.'

The policeman looked from one to the other, making his mind up. He finally declared he would require them to accompany him to Holborn Police Station. He would summon a station car. Was Mr. Hammond prepared to make his statement at the station?

And when Henry Hammond said yes, yes he was, the

policeman did some more thinking.

'I suggest,' interposed Henry Hammond, 'you allow me to telephone for a police car from Mr. Trematon's flat. It's just over there, you can see the lights on at the top of the building. In any case his sister will be wondering what has happened.'

'I will tell my own sister,' David said.

'Let us try not to be proprietory about this,' replied Henry Hammond easily; 'Anne's feelings are what matter.'

'Don't call her Anne,' said David.

'Miss Trematon,' said Henry Hammond, 'ought to know.'

This inspired the policeman to use his authority. He said it would be improper for Mr. Hammond to summon a car from Holborn Station. He must do that himself at the nearest telephone box. But it was quite in order that the lady be informed.

Henry Hammond moved to cross the road. 'I will tell her myself,' David said, and moved too. It was then apparent that Anne had forestalled them both; the street door beneath the flat stood open and she was out on the pavement, barely visible in the weak glow of the basement light behind her. She was looking up and down.

She saw them as they saw her, and she called out 'What has happened?'

Everybody foregathered on her side of the road. David wished she would look at him but she didn't. The policeman saw fit to assure her that nobody was under arrest. In greater agitation she repeated 'What has happened?' and he now told her 'These two persons are required for questioning in connection with an incident.'

She did not ask what the incident was. David read terrible misgiving in her face. But he said, 'It is all nonsense. Three friends came to supper with us. My sister will confirm what I say. Mr. Gedge and I saw them out of this door only a few minutes ago, and since then we have been talking about the stars.'

'Anne,' said Henry Hammond, 'I expect all will be well;

but the last part—under the stars so to speak—is the cause of the trouble, and that is the part which neither you nor I can confirm.'

'I know why you are here,' David shouted. It was the only time he shouted that evening. He had no idea why Henry Hammond was there. 'You are a filthy swine,' he said.

At once Anne warned him, 'David, you will do yourself harm talking like that.'

The policeman exclaimed 'Madam!' in a way that suggested agreement with her.

'I have changed my mind, officer,' said Henry Hammond then. 'I had not anticipated any such expression of ill will. I should prefer to make a statement here and now rather than at the police station; that seems the most effective way of helping those whom I still like to think of as my friends. And in fairness to myself I want it to be understood that I am not a spy. I want the whole thing out in the open. There is a sense in which I have been keeping watch, as you will hear. I may be a figure of fun. But I am not a spy. Nor have I intentionally brought harm on anyone.'

'You had better come inside,' said Anne quietly, and they followed her through the basement and upstairs to the flat. Anne drew the landing curtain. Otherwise everything was as it had been when Wack and the others were here.

The policeman asked Anne's permission to sit down, and only then removed his helmet. It occurred to David that he had taken her for much older than she was.

Anyhow she looked very pale.

She invited Mr. Gedge and Henry Hammond to sit down too, as if they were strangers. And then the policeman produced a notebook and a primitive form of ball-point pen, and asked Henry Hammond if he understood that his statement would be read back to him afterwards, and he must only sign it if it constituted a true record of what he had said.

Henry Hammond told his story in a low and stony voice. He said he was acutely embarrassed. He didn't look embarrassed to David. He looked a man who shielded a quite different emotion.

He studied the sleeves of his blue city suit and said he would not flinch from making himself appear ridiculous. He said he was here on purpose. He had been standing outside in the road, and had been standing there since much earlier this evening. He had stood in the road not every night but most nights recently. Breathing his words upon the policeman, Henry Hammond said he loved the lady of the house. Thus, outside in the dark, he could be near her. It was the only way. He could watch the lighted windows. He had caught a glimpse of her occasionally.

'The time passes quickly, I compose poems to her.'

To David this was a most cunning declaration.

'You will appreciate, officer,' said Henry Hammond, 'I find it painful to reveal feelings of such a private nature and, to me, supreme importance. I do so in order to explain my presence. It would not have been necessary, I would have said nothing about it, if Miss Trematon's brother with whom, you must understand, I am on Christian name terms, had not astonished me by imputing a hostile motive.'

'He is pretending,' David said.

The policeman said David would have an opportunity later to make his own statement.

'He knows I hate him,' David said.

Anne said, 'It's very late already, I don't think I can stand much more of this.'

'I tell you what,' said Mr. Gedge.

They all looked at him. He had been silent so long.

'What?' Anne asked him absently.

'I forget,' he said.

There was a pause.

David saw Henry Hammond catch the policeman's eye and, with an expressionless look, touch his forehead with his fingertip.

'Mr. Gedge is getting well after an illness,' said David. 'He is well now really. Some people tell lies about him.' He spoke at large.

'At the back of my mind—' Mr. Gedge began, then broke off and exclaimed 'There's a fossilised metaphor! We picture consciousness nowadays as a sea surface with an underneath to it, but the old metaphor goes on insisting on a drawer with a front and a back. At the back of my mind —my pre-Freudian filing cabinet—what shall we say?—oh I am ready for bed—I'm thinking about the language of pain in these situations which become unbearable—like holding your breath—but cannot be said to hurt. What shall we say? Oh what *shall* we say?'

'To hurt,' Anne prompted him.

'Now I remember!' he cried in a single rush of energy. 'I was going to tell you—that was it—I was going to say I can't stand much more of this either.'

The policeman asked Henry Hammond to continue, and to be as brief as possible; and Henry Hammond said he had been watching the windows of the flat when his attention was drawn to a disturbance in the middle of the road of all places. He could make out two figures. One was apparently threatening or cajoling the other. 'The more *passive* one' —with the faintest possible stress—'the slightly built one'— and a cool smile at David—'he seemed reluctant and perhaps even in trouble. How stupid of me not to put two and two together! I was anxious for him. When his companion drew him into that dark cavern of a passage, I feared an assault. Or worse. The street was quite deserted. I had no doubt that the right course of action was to summon help, preferably a policeman, before things went any further. It never crossed my mind they were star-gazing.'

He hesitated.

'Literally star-gazing,' he said.

Which to David at that moment was an unbearable taunt. The policeman tried to stop him but he waved him aside and told Henry Hammond he was a liar and a vulgar cheat who lived in a block of council flats and pretended to be smart. 'The whole family are as common as dirt,' David said.

Anne told him to stop and said she was ashamed of him. This cut him to the heart but he went on. The policeman intervened again. Even so he got it said that Henry Hammond must have seen him and Mr. Gedge saying goodnight to the other three. 'He knew from the start who we were. He is pretending. He is making it all up.'

Then David stopped. He felt self-refuted. Obviously Henry Hammond was not making it all up. Not it all. The middle of the road. The dark entrance. He remembered his fingers being opened.

From ages ago it seemed, from Hyde Park, the words 'Play fair now! No facts!' filled his head and he turned to meet the present gaze of those wonderful brown eyes.

'Lend me your handkerchief, my pretty,' said Mr. Gedge.

This might have been compromising once upon a time but not now, David thought, and never again, for when one's friend sweats painfully one helps in any small way one can, or big way for that matter.

Mr. Gedge wiped his brow and dabbed his cheeks and chin and upper lip.

'Keep it,' David said, to tell the world what's mine is his.

'Will you kindly finish your statement, sir,' the policeman asked Henry Hammond.

But Henry Hammond replied he had finished, that was all, and when the policeman referred him to what he called the incident, he replied again that he had no more to say.

'Perhaps the lady will excuse us if you and I step outside,' the policeman suggested.

Henry Hammond cleared his throat and said, 'I cannot be absolutely certain as to what I saw. Therefore, where there is room for doubt, however small, and where my personal feelings are so deeply involved, I must claim the right to keep silent.'

The policeman tried once more. He got as far as 'Let's put it this way, sir,' when Henry Hammond raised a hand against further discussion and declared he had put it to himself each and every way. There was no more to be said.

'Heaven knows, I am not trying to protect my own interest,' he added almost in a whisper. 'After this lamentable story of hanging about in the dark, why should I bother?'

Anne said it wasn't lamentable.

He murmured something about a laughing stock and comic opera lovers. 'Anyhow it's nice of you,' he then said out loud, and looked her in the face.

What a subtle foe! thought David, but he could find no words to enter with and wreck these careful advancing plans. He had never seen a policeman's helmet indoors before. He thought how large it was on their carpet. Then he sought Mr. Gedge's eyes again. They were shut. He got up and firmly woke his friend in case somebody else should startle him.

Still standing, David said, 'We told the truth. We were looking at the stars and then we were saying goodnight. We have done nothing wrong, so leave us alone. Mr. Gedge is staying with us and he must go to bed. Having been ill, he gets tired easily.'

The policeman asked if Mr. Gedge was a permanent resident.

Anne said no.

David told the policeman to mind his own business.

The policeman said it was his business and cautioned David against obstructing the course of justice.

'Sit down, David,' Anne urged him.

'At least let us be rational,' Henry Hammond said, while David remained standing. 'Just because something unfortunate has happened we need not all come out losers by it.'

That's meaningful, thought David, held back by a thread of prudence from saying he would rather everybody lost than Henry Hammond won.

In any case it wasn't as simple as that.

There was Mr. Gedge.

'Don't you agree with me, Anne?' asked Henry Hammond.

She did not answer.

Henry Hammond leaned forward to include them all except Mr. Gedge and said, as if puzzled, 'I might never have made such a stupid mistake if I had not felt certain our friend was still in hospital. There *was* something familiar about those wild gesticulations, those all-embracing gestures, even in the dark. But he was the last person I expected to find here. You see, the doctor in charge of his case warned me when I was considering possible jobs for him that there were dangers to be feared in a return to ordinary society, both now and for some time to come. But specially now.'

'It's all lies about jobs, you are a sort of clerk with no influence,' David told him.

'And yet even if I had known he was staying here, I suppose I might still have failed to interpret the signs correctly. After all, people living in the same house don't usually go out into the street to say goodnight.'

'You said he was not a permanent resident?' the policeman asked quickly, like a man whose duty is coming clear to him.

'He leaves us tomorrow,' said Anne.

'Back to the—er—hospital?'

'No.'

'Where is he going?'

Piercingly Mr. Gedge called out 'It's a secret.' Then in the silence he had created he said, 'David knows.'

Henry Hammond laughed and said 'Why should David know and nobody else?'

Anne rushed in with 'I have got a rough idea what is happening tomorrow,' but David was already bent upon some full affirmation. He turned on his sister and commanded her 'You will keep our secret.' The Reverend Crumm, Mrs. Crumm, the shed at the bottom of the garden—Mrs. Crumm specially, he had not met her but he could guess—and whatever a potting-shed was—the long garden—it all gave urgent sense to Mr. Gedge's words; and David, still on his feet, stood over Henry Hammond and told him he knew all about where Mr. Gedge was going, what he was doing from now on in his life, because he and he were true friends.

'Evidently,' Henry Hammond said.

David chose a place and struck him, but inexpertly, high on the side of the head above the ear.

'This is no flattery, as Shakespeare says,' called Mr. Gedge.

The policeman stood up.

David felt suddenly sick. He decided not to strike again. His eyes were swimming, he could scarcely see anyway.

'Tooth and claw, David,' said Henry Hammond in newly discovered warm tones. 'You know I wanted it otherwise.' Then he addressed the policeman. 'I suppose the time has come to say over to you, officer,' he said.

Anne, who had been leaning back in her chair, got up almost briskly and went into her bedroom. As soon as he had watched her go the policeman brought things to an end. He would not require David at the station. There was an insufficiency of evidence regarding the incident. Unless, he said, Mr. Hammond chose to add to his statement. But he must require this person—Mr. Gedge—to accompany him. 'Why?' said David. 'On account of various items,' said the policeman. He refused to say what items. 'Then we will refuse to go with you,' said David. 'There is no we about it, you are not being asked to go,' said Henry Hammond. 'If Mr. Gedge goes I go with him,' said David. 'Something tells me he will be going,' said Henry Hammond.

29

'SHE said I wanted the moon. My music and her at home always to look after me—no she said that wasn't fair, she took it back, she said I was her loving considerate brother often—and now Mr. Gedge, and one day sooner or later, probably sooner, I would meet a girl and want her too.'

'Everybody of eighteen who is anybody wants the moon,' said Mr. Turgoose. 'Fuck me,' he added with nostalgia.

'She said one must learn to choose in life.'

'Or to compromise?'

'She said choose.'

'The ones who are going to remain anybody certainly learn something,' Mr. Turgoose said. 'Perhaps they do the choosing and leave the compromising to chronic small-timers like me. The paper has just been bought up. We aren't profitable. They've got us by the short and curly, and I haven't even met the new editor. It makes my balls ache to think I have been licking the wrong boots all these years.'

'She said one must choose, one can't have everything. I know I'm selfish but I don't find choosing any easier when I'm being unselfish. I'm not like her. Going for different things at once seems to be part of being happy. I mean it doesn't feel wicked. She goes to church of course, and I stopped long ago.'

Hastily, Mr. Turgoose said, 'Don't you start the church habit again. It won't help. Unless you really feel like it.'

David tried to collect his thoughts about religion and feeling like it.

'Still,' said Mr. Turgoose, 'she can say this and a lot more without walking out on you.'

'She won't walk out,' David assured him, 'she will stay. She is going to help me find somewhere to share with Colin Innes.'

'Your celloist, you said?'

'Cellist.'

'Your cellist.'

'No, viola.'

'That could be nice,' Mr. Turgoose reflected. He did not speak entirely without conviction, but his 'could' sank deep and was desolating. And deeper still, David groped after his reason for being certain it was a bad idea to share with Colin. More than an idea. It was going to happen.

The quartet joined religion and feeling like it in his dull turmoil of considerations.

'No it couldn't,' he said finally. 'It will hurt our music.'

He sat very still and tried to think.

'Drink up, old pal,' Mr. Turgoose urged.

David sipped the recommended light ale. It contained little alcohol, so Mr. Turgoose had assured him, and he spoke the truth. David was not drunk but there was something wrong in his head which prevented him thinking. He supposed it was being unhappy, but very very unhappy, and lost. And tired of course. It never occurred to him to blame his purple medicine—not then and not until long afterwards when he happened to merit a severe warning from his doctor against mixing drink, even a little drink, and barbiturates. That was it! he realised or anyhow he more or less believed, in nineteen sixty whatever it was; and he cherished, momentarily, a ghost of long-buried revenge and restoration: Dr. Hennessy's negligence exposed at last, public shame for him, the case of Mr. Gedge reconsidered, a new start for David too, his talent cleansed and faults forgiven—in fact he embarrassed himself by his middle-aged dream of the world made young again when, stepping out of that other, later doctor's surgery, he saw things as they were, which is to say as they appeared, a woman in fact with her little dog, two lives joined together by a witless strip of leather.

'I call it crying over spilt milk.'

'What?'

'Your sister. Making this fuss when the poor old genius is back where he came from and there's hells all to do about it.'

'He isn't really old.'

'Anyhow,' said Mr. Turgoose.

'She didn't make a fuss until I had gone on trying to persuade her to change her mind. I told her it was all finished, Mr. Gedge would never come out again, and she and I would be as we always had been. I said how sorry I was. I kept on saying sorry. Again and again. I said let's forget.'

'Give her a surprise.'

David puzzled for a moment.

'Take her home some flowers.'

'We aren't like that.'

'All girls are like that. Believe you me.'

'Not Anne. Not with me. I think I had better tell you exactly what happened.'

'Then hang on a sec, friend of my youth,' said Mr. Turgoose, 'while I replenish;' and he carried his glass to the saloon bar, smoky and small and dark and quiet compared with bars in later times, and yet it was crowded so that he joined almost a queue.

He turned to give a Thumbs Up sign showing he would not be long.

David still could not think, but he was calmer. The walking-stick beside Mr. Turgoose's chair was a help. It lay there. He appraised its form and wondered why now of all times he liked being called old pal and things like that which were untrue. Oh God. He gripped the arms of his own chair for firmness. I suppose it's the shock, he told himself. Delayed shock.

What should someone do who doesn't believe in God?

Pray to Jesus who really lived?

Really lived.

Play fair now! no facts.

It's hard, David thought, much too hard when I'm only me. But I know I loved him.

He remembered Mr. Gedge asking them to pause under the stars and observe Andromeda. 'She has moved, you see,' he told the three policemen, 'since I was teaching David how to find her. We have so much to bear in mind.' The two new policemen wore flat caps. They came in a car when the first policeman telephoned.

They asked David, did he understand he was under no compulsion? They were very insistent. So was the inspector who talked to him at Holborn Police Station. He thanked him for this voluntary assistance and began questioning him about what they were doing when they were found. He too talked about their posture. Mr. Gedge was being questioned somewhere else and David described everything as it happened, the complete truth.

He felt sure this was the wisest course.

'You are clear that he bent down for that specific purpose?' the inspector asked. 'One might have expected him to raise your hand to his lips.'

David said nothing.

'Did it strike you as an unusual posture?'

And when David still said nothing the inspector told him 'Just consider this question on its own.'

David then answered, 'Let me explain.' He said it was no good trying to understand anything on its own. That was why he was here, he had come to make sure they got the whole picture. Otherwise they might easily reach a wrong conclusion about Mr. Gedge. For Mr. Gedge was a philosopher, 'He is a great man in my opinion,' said David, and like many philosophers he was eccentric, he had mannerisms; but among other philosophers and artists and musicians, people who understood and admired him, and ordinary people for that matter, he was not too eccentric. David told the inspector about the last three days, how good they had been. It was absolutely vital the inspector should not spoil everything now. Whatever happened he must not treat Mr. Gedge as if he suspected him of being a criminal, or insane. Mr. Gedge would not be able to stand it. He might appear calm and firm, though eccentric, and even in a joking mood part of the time, 'but I know he cannot bear much more of this,' David concluded.

'What makes you say that?' the inspector asked.

David caught the yawn in his voice. It was obvious he had his own views and was only sparing the tip of his attention to listen and speak with.

'I know because he told me.'

'If I were you I would take everything he told me with a pinch of salt.'

Then the inspector sent his eyes on a special mission over the surface of David's face, and said, 'I would go further than that. I would have nothing more to do with him.'

'Where is he?'

David really meant he refused to be kept apart from him any longer.

'We are taking care of that,' the inspector said.

'He and I have work to do. Together. We must go home. What is more we have friends in common. We are all meeting this Sunday if you want to know.'

The inspector replied in facetious American, 'There ain't gonna be no Sunday.'

'For him,' he added in his own voice.

For him.

Something jerked David back into the present. He watched Mr. Turgoose limp busily along the bar. A war wound? Mr. Turgoose limped in pursuit of a soda syphon.

It has happened, David thought, it can't unhappen; I said I would describe, I will describe exactly what happened when he comes back with his drink, but it can't unhappen, it's advice I want, I must pick out the bits which have some connection with the future, if there are any and what future? the inspector said I was at liberty to remain saying however it was pointless, a long wait and a policeman more like a fisherman in his blue pullover brought a small hours duty mug of tea before the scream eternal scream until I found him where they had taken his gloves off, a frequent place of concealment say drugs the police doctor said, I found my friend not a friend my mad friend and his clothes fouled obviously—but I have a thing about smells or I would have done better and again when the same fisherman duty policeman called to me running out he knew the type, they were artful how they approached young fellows, he said he saw what I needed, I was normal, he betted I could find a keyhole in the dark if it had fur round it.

This was is still today, at the hospital 'The end of the road, I meant what I said.' 'You allowed me to see him last time.' 'The medical circumstances were different.' 'Then let me see your wife, she will understand.'

And this afternoon, the Reverend Crumm, 'We'll say a little prayer for him,' and thanked me for coming, he was glad to be told and no we won't bother Gwen, he will put the potting-shed to rights.

Mr. Turgoose knows about women although she is my sister. I will ask him, I will put it in a general way like a problem. If a woman, or girl, says 'I know you are sorry but it will go on happening,' what then? Go on happening means a future but the same thing can't go on happening to people who aren't together for it to happen to, and can it happen to them separately without becoming a different thing? but it might be the same thing but end differently if only she would let it go on happening to the people while they were still together so if a third person were to come and be made very welcome who had been struck on the head for example which was why apologising how to say it needed careful thought going there and walk up and down where he lived and a bit quite a long way round to think a battered green van the same one and Saloon Bar if Mister I forget is inside his advice...

'Oh I am glad to meet you.'

'I can see you are—as the girl said to the young man in

the nudist camp. Here. Steady, old pal. Easy now. Easy. What's up? Count up to ten—no, never mind, don't try and tell me now. Let's have some fresh air. We'll come back when we've taken a turn.'

A turn.

And another turn.

'And then what did she say?'

'She said I wanted the moon. My music and her at home always to look after me—no she said that wasn't fair, she took it back, she said I was her loving considerate brother often—and now Mr. Gedge, and one day sooner or later, probably sooner, I would meet a girl and want her too.'

'Everybody of eighteen who is anybody wants the moon,' said Mr. Turgoose.

30

AND now, the Reverend Crumm serves the same God but a different flock whose improvement, he always swears, comes from using his loaf, or (when he expresses it less slangily) from his being blessed with that extra something, that kink of imagination.

He is referring to the greengages and cherry tarts.

He had this idea—how like him! individualist that he is!—he had it when everybody else was turning dead against the whole principle of uniform, and the ties and caps were in danger of being swept away along with the rest, as a Victorian relic. The facts are these. From the year dot the men getting ready for church, the church party that is, have worn scarlet neckties, and the women, green knitted caps which hang slightly below the ears and which in earlier days gave the Hall barber his female norm as regards length and general style.

Once in church they sit separately of course; and it was this little circumstance, green in the north aisle here and red here in the south, that led the Reverend Crumm one inspired Sunday morning years ago, a mid-winter morning, frost had made the ground tacky underfoot, to arouse their latent pride in themselves, their desire for competition. He instituted his points system.

When that storm broke over uniform, the management committee was bound to include the caps and ties in its deliberations. The Reverend Crumm was ready. Somebody might force a vote. He expected a shemozzle. He held his fire and then he let them have it with both barrels. 'I suggest you come with me,' he said, 'and see for yourselves —those of you who entertain no scruple about darkening the doors of a church.'

Strong stuff.

It was Whitsun. The greengages had decorated their aisle with crêpe paper done in orange flutes and darts of pente-costal flame. Round the pillars.

Very nice. Very suggestive. Four points out of a possible five.

The south aisle was bare.

'But here,' the Reverend Crumm said, 'this is a bit of a facer.'

Members of the management committee followed him up the nave to the pulpit, and found it adorned with a single neatly divided ox's tongue.

'Tell tale tit,' murmured Lady Sloan, the only woman present.

Cyril was responsible. A prominent cherry tart, Cyril worked in the Hall kitchen whenever he was well enough.

The chairman of the management committee asked in genuine wonder, 'What will you do?'

'Two points out of five,' said the Reverend Crumm. A setback for the cherry tarts. But one had to watch it like a hawk or they got discouraged. He added, there were always means of ensuring one team did not fall too far behind the other. The really important thing was to give a rational explanation for lost points, and above all an explanation which they could fathom. Tricky of course, but tremend-ously worthwhile. Next Sunday he must go over the Whit-sun epistle again. They were sure to pitch into him—the more lively cherry tarts—not just Cyril—over the cloven tongues like as of fire. Had members of the committee noticed how literal-minded small boys were, compared with girls? It was the same in second childhood and mental ill-ness generally. He would have to mind his Ps and Qs when they came back at him, as he knew they would, saying it actually mentioned tongues in the descent of the Holy Ghost. Acknowledging Lady Sloan, he observed 'Women have a more intuitive grasp of symbolism.'

'I'm a bit of a cherry tart myself,' said the chairman of the management committee, 'in this respect.'

'And if the women want to know what has happened to their fifth point, you said four out of five?' asked a member.

The Reverend Crumm noted his spiteful smile and said nothing.

Still regarding the ox-tongue, Lady Sloan stated, regretfully, 'It will attract mice.'

Another said, 'Surely one can stimulate and maintain a healthy rivalry without having recourse to institutional badges which smack of the bad old days of the Commissioners in Lunacy? Modern opinion, as I was saying at our meeting, is unanimous about this, and it seems to me vitally important to recognise which is the progressive attitude, and to adopt it.'

'We have had our disappointments,' the Reverend Crumm declared rather inconsequentially, almost shouting. The empty building rang. Then, struggling with increasing success against his scorn, he began a long speech. 'Badges. People jaw a lot nowadays about what is progressive and what is reactionary. You hear it everywhere. These have become jargon terms, if I may say so. Anything can be laughed at. It depends how you look at it. Nothing goes forward all the time. Badges reminds me, I don't know if you will call it reactionary—can you read what's in my mind, I wonder?—badges reminds me of regimental pride...'

That was some years ago now. As we know, the Reverend Crumm carried the day in the set-to over the caps and ties Morale was high—it still is—but he fairly threw himself into the fray when he was new at Shardingley. The time seems to have flown since the days when the young people in our story thought of him as an old man. Now he really is old, and he often reviews his life as if it were complete, and logical. Nevertheless he can make no human sense of his move to Shardingley. He has to say God short-changed him. What makes him laugh is that he imagined coming to Shardingley would force him to develop his scholarly, contemplative side. He supposed it would be so quiet.

When Gwen died very suddenly, on holiday, he supposed the mood of elation which seized him was hysterical. He waited for it to go and the suffering to start. He returned to Finchley and waited. But it didn't go. Or rather, it settled down into an apparently self-renewing peace. He slept like a log. Our marriage, all those years, has become a sort of favourite poem, he thought, visiting her grave a few months later; and I'm not lonely, I don't mind roughing it in the Rectory, I love these London streets and coming home absolutely whacked and drawing the curtains, getting the fire going and then a spot of supper. The midnight desk work, the alarm-clock, the early start. He caught flu that winter and thought aha, but friends rallied round. And then one morning he was shaving in his bath—a youthful habit he had returned to—he drove a first swathe through the lather with his faithful old cut-throat and was preparing a second; he was resolving to speak to the daily woman about the cobwebs and dirt in here, one mustn't tempt them to slack, they reckon single men are easy game— he was seeking exactness in the steamy mirror which stood propped against the soap-rack, when he caught a fleeting devil in his eye. He regarded himself long and strangely but learnt no more. This is the fright I used to ask for, he interpreted. My immortal soul! And he laid the razor flat against his already white throat whiskers.

He upped and went to the first remote country living that fell vacant, Shardingley in South Derbyshire. Before he left he joined the London Library for books by post, and began to ponder a long postponed ambition, a Commentary on Romans, *Contre Karl Barth* as he provisionally, half humorously entitled it.

His German was rusty and his New Testament Greek was no great shakes either.

But how much has that got to do with my soul? he found

himself asking in next to no time, after the extraordinary killing at Shardingley Hall.

James Dyer and John Benson were two quiet middle-aged men who had worked together for many years. Dyer shovelled dung into Benson's wheelbarrow, and Benson wheeled the dung from the main heap to the kitchen garden and then returned for more. (They did the same sort of thing with coal and coke.) One day—the Reverend Crumm had arrived at the parish literally the week before —Benson was stooping to grasp the handles of his full barrow when Dyer struck him from behind with his shovel and killed him. It seemed there was no quarrel.

Benson's sister wanted to discuss the funeral. She was evidently distraught although she had not visited her brother in twenty years. The Reverend Crumm gave her a stiff drink and listened. We can imagine his state of mind. He had never heard of Shardingley Hall, and he would have avoided this particular parish like the plague if he had; and there the place was, half a mile across the fields and not much more by road.

And here was the dead man's sister.

In for a penny in for a pound, he quickly decided.

Even today the church party is only a small fraction of the population of the Hall. There are whole wards and corridors where the scorched sweet incontinent air never stirs. Some howl all day. Some sit and weep silently. Some wear padded head-guards, a cross between football and boxing, to mitigate epileptic tumbles, to protect misshapen scarred heads like balloons that have been blown up too long. The Reverend Crumm will never forget entering for the first time by a side door and being reminded of the Golders Green Model Laundry where he always had a girl or two to visit. He got lost. It is a huge place. Now he knows it inside out. Very little positive cruelty goes on there, but much neglect. How could it be otherwise when the Hall is largely staffed by foreigners who work in shifts, West Indians, Pakistanis, sleepy Spaniards, Irish men and women, much seasonal labour—it comes and goes in mini-buses between the Hall and Loughborough, Derby, Nottingham and other big towns?

He does what he can. Sometimes it seems very little. But the church party is twice what it was when he arrived, mentally as well as in numbers. 'We have strengthened our top storey,' as he tells visitors, though there are few of those. The greengages and cherry tarts virtually are his congregation, and, thanks to the points system, Shardingley parish church is kept like a new pin.

There is not a Mothers Union for miles round that can match the best of the Reverend Crumm's greengages in embroidery. The altar linen and vestments are a sight for sore eyes.

More or less level pegging, however, is ensured for the cherry tarts. Only the other day four of them carried a piano without putting it down once, from the Hall to the church, and it will have to go back. All the heavy work is their responsibility, and tending the churchyard. They are clamouring to be allowed to dig graves. The Reverend Crumm has decided to let them. He remembers James Dyer and John Benson, and keeps his fingers crossed.

Naturally little things go wrong all the time.

Only this morning Cyril—the same Cyril—too old for kitchen work now—our friend Cyril forgot to ring the matins bell.

'Minus one point,' says the Reverend Crumm.

'Minus two, Reverend,' cries an excited greengage.

'Plus one,' retorts Mr. Gedge; 'all cherry tarts are proud of Cyril. He is our first no bell prizeringer.'

They are going at it hammer and tongs; this is the time set aside by the Reverend Crumm each Sunday morning, and make no mistake, arguing out plus and minus points can lead to acrimony. He likes to have it all finished before the service starts so they can say the Lord's Prayer together and begin with a clean slate.

A duffer like Cyril needs a long-stop, thinks the Reverend

216

Crumm—someone to stand ready in case he forgets. It's a miracle he hasn't done so before. We must find somebody smart for long-stop.

Mr. Gedge himself?

It might keep him quiet. Or quieter. Not too quiet or we may lose him again.

He has been a cherry tart for over a year now. Which is not long compared with his entire time at the Hall, of course. But hopes run high.

But beware! a strong tormenting wind!

Envisage him before church at his usual task of litter collection in the grounds of the Hall. He wields a Neptune's trident, a monstrous toasting-fork to impale paper on, and in an old, old headline he learns that three men have reached the moon, a trivial, a routine development, but alas he reads on to where the President declares nothing so important has happened since the world began.

What shall we say?

Almost dark.

Bang! bang! bang! go the nails in the ark our coffin if that arkyoumeant holds water.

What shall we answer?—clutching his testicles, a common senile attitude—goodness what shall we say?

It must enter two by two by now by ark he means his file.

Unspike the President.

Gingerly he frees the brittle yellow paper and carries those words home.

Oh how difficult he finds the life of thought sometimes, though as a rule the file helps him to be in no hurry but on the contrary to think always at thought's pace since the meaning of the world must lie outside the world and here for the most part we are, as he opens the file, releases the spring and places the President on top of the appeal to the housewife *Ask the men in your family* before you buy lavatory paper, *Ask the men,* father in the photograph and

217

little son float a model boat and paddle back view, those perceptive male bottoms, transcendental aesthetic which Kant child of his time never dreamed of, and Mr. Gedge hugs the file gratefully to him aware that his own metaphysic of naming was also tainted with history, how fortunate it never got published, he was once a child of his time too.

'Gedgy, overalls off. Tie on. Church parade.'

This tree, as the cherry tarts pass underneath, is the tree the squirrel dropped from (they do fall occasionally, profound mortal gesture, and might even if they didn't) and bit Mr. Gedge's finger pat before she died. Which finger? which reminds him we were sure blood flowed in the rice crispies but Cyril only forgot which way having circumcised our breakfast tomato juice cans which way hup two three four skins and naval surgeons how they specialise.

Mr. Gedge's file, but walking also fosters the life of thought until he concludes 'The middle decades of that century were language-mad, and let me whisper in your ear I was afflicted myself—and now, what a lovely day! the true sublime considering red and beautiful have the same root in Russian' he tells his neighbour who has been saying and now repeats nothing will persuade him to undress in front of a lady announcer—*faute demure* in Mr. Gedge's opinion, no public shame, no cry *de profumis*. Nevertheless they must place a screen before the television set until Arthur Pitt calls himself decent tonight and every night.

The medical superintendent has advised Arthur Pitt to make the lady announcer his girl friend. Therefore he informs Mr. Gedge as they walk churchwards together 'Between ourselves, I dislike our host,' by whom Mr. Gedge understands the Reverend Crumm, replying 'We must take him as we find him, stigmata and all,' displaying a white scar on a brown finger.

'And there's my voice to think of,' says Arthur Pitt. For he has a solo ahead of him.

He keeps silent, saving his voice while they arrive at the

porch and are welcomed and mingle momentarily with the greengages, and silent throughout the weekly points session in the vestry.

The Reverend Crumm tells Arthur Pitt to keep his pecker up, having decided he is nervous. They talk alone, a few words after the Lord's Prayer and while the greengages file into the pews of the north aisle here, and the cherry tarts here to the south. 'I know that D-Day feeling, Arthur,' says the Reverend Crumm, and as he speaks his gaze wanders over familiar green and red, the wrinkled witty faces, the dry eyeballs and fluttering hands. How the years flash by! he thinks, and then he supposes every old man thinks that. This is the sort of weather that rouses old memories.

And the years are also beginning to stand still.

He announces Hymn 178.

'Verse Three—Verse *Three* is Arthur's verse.'

They have been told before, this has been the talk of the week, and they are mostly ready when Verse Three comes. The organ stops. Arthur Pitt sings unaccompanied in a braying head voice with lavish snarling *portamenti*, for he once owned a plum-label record of Caruso singing Toselli's famous Serenade. He sings:

> *Or if I stray, he doth convert,*
> *And brings my mind in frame,*
> *And all this not for my desert,*
> *But for his holy name.*

'Well, God must be amazed at Arthur,' says the Reverend Crumm.

There is talk and scattered applause.

Will reason silence folly? grows bolder in Mr. Gedge's head. He has returned to the President's mad opinion, and now the music and he knows, he knows from his litter collection, he knows and has it safe in the file: there is a racehorse called Beethoven, these horrors are with us, and he looks along the seated cherry tarts and can't see any David

where old acquaintance is always playing with its buttons
in chaste mutuality in the eye of God's policeman's torch

'A light to lighten the genitals.'

'Minus one point, Reverend,' cries a greengage.

Chiefly to Mr. Gedge who is smiling, his head on his left
shoulder, his tongue visible but not his sticky mortar of
images he fights for reason among—to him and to all cherry
tarts, the Reverend Crumm declares, 'Because Arthur sang
so beautifully, don't imagine you have a bagful of points
to spare. Remember Poppy Day!'

A shrewd stroke. Abashed cherry tarts remind each other
of a certain event, a slipping out and getting the Bishop's
car started with the wire core of a poppy and driving it to
Burton upon Trent.

And bishop reminds the Reverend Crumm. People from
outside will not realise (he tells himself with heat) how literal-minded my tarts are. He would like to show the Bishop
their wind machine, a wooden box like a loud-speaker waiting to go back to the Hall workshop. Mercifully it never
worked. Everything passed off quietly. Pentecost has been
and gone again, and by next year they will have forgotten
their wind machine and everything he told them of the
wealth of symbolism in that one little *as* when they were
reading together *And suddenly there came a sound from
heaven as of a rushing mighty wind, and it filled all the
house where they were sitting*. Thank goodness it didn't
work. He doesn't mind admitting he kept his fingers crossed
while Raymond was shaking out the flex and preparing to
switch on. All went well. Were the lupins early this year,
or was Whitsun late? A quite outstanding greengage has
charge of altar decoration these days. Her flowers, this lot,
her pentecostal lupins, are past their best, but their tor-
tured pink and white rhythm is more flamelike than ever.
They twist as they grow old. Like us. A charming touch.

Freud! thinks the Reverend Crumm a trifle stiffly. He
could do with a breather but there's no peace for the
wicked. Mary Reynolds has stuffed her hassock up under her

skirt, and is caressing the bump. For the umpteenth time. She usually sorts herself out, so he decides to leave it and announces the Lesson. 'Priscilla is going to read us the story of the Good Samaritan,' he says.

A hymn and now a lesson. What sort of matins is this?

The occasional visitor to Shardingley may well wonder. The service consists of the hymn we have just had, a lesson, a short sermon, a few prayers, a final hymn, the blessing. Psalms and canticles, the Reverend Crumm decided long ago, are tricky and (not to put too fine a point on it) bad for morale. Experience also shows that a second lesson spoils the effect of the first. The creed has been the one controversial omission; nobody up at the Hall cared a hoot one way or the other, but there must have been talk in the village, he had the Bishop breathing down his neck before he could say Jack Robinson.

A mere boy.

While Priscilla reads, and reads almost faultlessly, the Reverend Crumm congratulates himself on the idea of Arthur Pitt's solo; but for that he would have been hard put to it to maintain level pegging.

Priscilla reads, 'And likewise a Levite, when he was at the place, came and looked on him, and passed by on the other side. But a certain Samaritan, as he journeyed, came where he was; and, when he saw him, he had compassion on him, and went to him, and bound up his wounds, pouring in oil and wine, and set him on his own beast, and brought him to an inn, and took care of him. And on the morrow, when he departed, he took out two pence and gave them to the host—'

'Not enough,' declares an unidentified voice, a cherry tart's of course.

If the Bishop were here he would soon see sense about the creed, when some of us even manage to foozle the Samaritan.

'Listen!' says Priscilla Dawes severely. She knows the gospel apart from having prepared her lesson. '—and said unto him, Take care of him; and whatsoever thou spendest more, when I come again, I will repay thee. Which now of these three, thinkest thou, was neighbour unto him that fell among the thieves?'

She pauses and looks about her, and Susan Fletcher who also knows the good book answers, 'He that shewed mercy on him,' and Mr. Gedge crosses a sudden lucid avenue where mercy and justice meet in the Hebrew word which escapes him but no matter, the husband of Christ's mother is being merciful, *being a just man and not willing to make her a public example*, when he knows no more than she is pregnant and not by him, and not by me (affirms Mr. Gedge as darkness comes again) when they held her head, she was trembling, and forced her small fastidious feet her pretty legs into two pairs of seaboots and mounted her, mare's tail plucked up, and one and one and one and one and one and one and one no fun—

We must watch him, thinks the Reverend Crumm, watching him, watching him watching—or we will lose him again.

—no rum, disgrace to our good name ashore and no rum punishes seven for antagonising Shetland farmers while the trick cyclist's report pends on Sailmaker Gedge, and when the navy says go...

'Buggers can't be choosers.'

'Minus another point, Reverend.'

'We will deal with that in a minute, Mary. Arthur—you are in sparkling form today—will you take our dear friend, our neighbour, I will be talking about neighbours in a minute—will you take him for a little walk. It's a beautiful day—'

'Minus one and minus one makes minus two, Reverend.'

'In a minute, Mary. In a minute. We will put that straight in a minute.'